Psyche

Herbert G. de Lisser

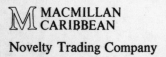

MACMILLAN CARIBBEAN

Novelty Trading Company

This edition first published 1980
Reprinted 1985

Published by *Macmillan Publishers Ltd*
London and Basingstoke
*Associated companies and representatives in Accra,
Auckland, Delhi, Dublin, Gaborone, Hamburg, Harare,
Hong Kong, Kuala Lumpur, Lagos, Manzini, Melbourne,
Mexico City, Nairobi, New York, Singapore, Tokyo*

Published for
The Novelty Trading Company Ltd
Jamaica

ISBN 0 333 29439 4

Printed in Hong Kong

By the same author
Morgan's Daughter
The White Witch of Rosehall

CONTENTS

BOOK ONE

Chapter		Page
1	PSYCHE	9
2	OLD THINGS AND NEW	18
3	ACCOMPLISHMENT	26
4	THE NET IS SPREAD	32
5	A VISIT TO PLIMSOLE	40
6	JOSEPHINE WINS	47
7	AT THE GREAT HOUSE	52
8	PSYCHE DECIDES	57
9	FAILURE OR SUCCESS?	65
10	AT LAST	74
11	DESTINY	80
12	THE PROMISE	89

BOOK TWO

13	THE LETTER	99
14	HOMECOMING	108
15	REALISATIONS	116
16	DREGS OF BITTERNESS	127
17	PREPARATIONS	137
18	AT THE BAZAAR	145
19	THE MEETING	155
20	MR. MORTON'S VIEW	165
21	MR. MORTON INTERVENES	174
22	FRED'S DECISION	184
23	CHRISTMAS DAY	191
24	THE TERRIBLE LAUGH	201
25	FREDERICK	209
26	AS IT WAS IN THE BEGINNING	217

BOOK ONE

BOOK ONE

Chapter 1

PSYCHE

IT WAS still early morning. But on the slave ship in Kingston Harbour there had been great activity for some time before daybreak. The ship had dropped anchor in the forenoon of the previous day and at once the master and crew of her had begun preparing their human cargo for the sale that was to take place next morning; they were in a jovial frame of mind for not more than fifteen of the slaves had died on the long voyage from the West Coast of Africa to Jamaica, and the rest were, take it all in all, in very good condition indeed.

When the sun rose it shone on groups of human beings who had been brought up from the holds of the ship, bathed by having sea water liberally sluiced over them, and given a large breakfast of yams and boiled cornmeal dumplings. Practically all of these folk were young, since the age at which they should be taken from their homes had been fixed by law at not above twenty-five; but there were one or two older ones among them also, and especially remarkable among these was a giant who must have been fifty if a day and who was obviously regarded by the other slaves with marked respect.

But among the women it was a girl of not more than seventeen years of age who stood conspicuously out. She had been bathed and had been given some sort of a frock to cover her nakedness; this dress she had used as a kind of apron, so that her back was entirely exposed and her firm, prominent young breasts and well-proportioned torso bore not a vestige of covering.

Three or four metal anklets adorned her feet; on her arms she wore a few brass bangles. She was tall, with flashing

9

coal-black eyes, and held herself as though she considered she was someone of importance.

Of her the master and his officer had made a favourite during the voyage, hence she had fared very well. It is true that she slept down below with the other women, but she had received tit-bits from the officers' table, salted meat and boiled cornmeal, or maize, and often tea and coffee, and she had been taught many words of English as day followed day aboard the ship, showing as she pointed to this object and that, and repeated the names spoken to her by the Britishers, a quick intelligence which put her quite apart from her companions in misfortune.

'There's a strain of Arab blood in her,' the master had said more than once, glancing at her long hair and thin lips; 'she isn't the pure McKay.'

'Perhaps, sir,' had once ventured a junior officer, 'she is the daughter of a chief.'

'That's what every one of them will say after they have been a year in Jamaica,' laughed the captain; 'everybody wants to be the son or daughter of a chief. But being that would not give this girl the features and hair she has. No. I guess there's Arab blood in her though her complexion is quite black. She has longish, soft hair; then look at her nose; it is positively hooked.' (By this he meant that the girl's nose was more inclined to be aquiline than platerine or flat.) 'She's good-looking too. I ought to get a tidy sum for her.'

He spat tobacco juice over the rail upon which he was leaning, and resumed.

'She may even be a virgin, though at her age that would be rare in Africa. But somehow I don't think she was married, though not being married would not make her a virgin, of course. However, whatever she is, she will remain exactly so on my ship, by God, for I won't have that girl interfered with by my men. I'd half-kill anyone on this ship that I found monkeying with my profits.'

He had named the girl Psyche. Classical names for slaves

had become the fashion of late in the West Indies, and he
had heard of Psyche somewhere, though he could not have
said to whom it referred or from what language it came.
She had quickly grasped what her new name was, and
answered readily to it. And she had stuck to the old man,
as much as he would allow her to do so, on the voyage,
having instinctively understood that the younger white men
had been warned away from her and were perforce avoiding
her.

Now and then she would give one of them a quick glance,
which might have been taken as an invitation. But there
dared be no answer. The officers had long since learnt that
their chief combined a passion for profits with a terrible
temper when provoked, and he seemed to have eyes all
over his head. Yet they liked Psyche; her youth, her looks,
her manner, her spirit appealed to them. So for her, on the
whole, the voyage had been a very pleasant one.

On the narrow wooden pier that jutted out into the water
of Kingston Harbour a small crowd of men soon began to
appear. These were planters who had come into Kingston
a few days before to await the arrival of this ship. In trousers
of white drill, overtopped by tweed waistcoats and long
coats whose tails covered more than half the length of the
back of their legs, with feet cased in serviceable black boots,
and heads covered with broadrimmed beavers—a form of
dress quite unsuited to tropical conditions—they looked
smart enough but could not possibly be comfortable. Yet
to be clothed and hatted otherwise would have seemed to
them a derogation of rank on such an occasion. Show,
ostentation, was a necessity entailed upon them when they
visited Kingston, or any other important town of the island.
They were planters of position and this was the dress which
they expected each other to wear when they came to town.

The wharf from which the wooden rickety pier projected
into the still, shining harbour formed by a long spit of land
that ended at a narrow entrance miles away to the south,

was an unpaved oblong enclosure with a few low wooden
buildings in it; in this yard men clad in rough osnaburg
trousers and loose jackets of the same material were rolling
hogsheads into one of the buildings or warehouses of the
place. Behind lay the city, situated at the tip of a plain that
was backed by a great arc of mountains whose tops were
now hidden in vapour and mist which the rays of the rising
sun would shortly dissipate. Even from the deck of the slave
ship Kingston looked a congeries of mean buildings, low,
small, but each seemingly set in a garden of high trees which
at a distance relieved the ugliness of the town that had sprung
into existence shortly after the destruction of Port Royal by
earthquake over a hundred years before.

The planters on the pier could see distinctly who were on
the ship's deck in so far as the crowd of people standing there
allowed. Only about three hundred and fifty slaves had come
on a vessel which could carry five hundred men and women
in its spaces below deck, and perhaps six hundred at a pinch.
The white men, crew and officers, numbered about fifty.
But the purchasers did not go aboard; the selling of the
slaves would take place in a building within the wharf
premises set apart for that purpose. Yet the eyes of potential
purchasers were already busy scrutinising the men and
women who would shortly be disposed of by auction or by
bargaining, each of them intent upon provisionally selecting
beforehand those workers whom he thought he would prefer
if they passed the preliminary examination as to their health
and strength.

One young man glanced casually at the slaves while the
gangway was being run between the ship and pier, and his
eyes alighted on Psyche. She stood near the rail nearest to
the pier; she had been purposely placed there by the
captain as a sort of attraction. She was gazing earnestly on
the white men on the pier, exactly the like of whom she had
never seen before. Her eyes were caught by those of the
young planter but a few yards away. They stared at one

another. Then the young man's attention was momentarily distracted by the voice of someone speaking to him from behind.

The slaves now began to stream across the gangway, but as yet Psyche had not stirred. She had been made to understand by Captain McClintock (who spoke her dialect fairly well) that she must not move until ordered to do so. The eyes of the young man on the pier returned to her.

The man behind him noticed his preoccupation, followed the direction of his glance, and grinned. 'That's a fine-looking colt there,' he observed; 'thinking of buying her, sir?'

'I don't know, Jones; I might or I might not; it will all depend on her price.'

'If you don't, I think I will,' returned Mr. Jones; 'Golden Spring wants some hands, and some breeders among them. That girl should be able to bear many children, and if the trade stops we shall want every hand that is born in the island.'

Huntingdon nodded, and began to walk towards the auction house in the wharf where the slaves were to be sold. He was twenty-eight and had been some five years in the colony. He was a younger son, his father a nobleman who had given him his Jamaica estate, since the rest of the family property must go to the elder brother; he was the Hon. Charles Huntingdon, and in the northern part of the island where his estate was situated he had already won a reputation for kindness to his bondspeople.

The ground of the wharf's yard was rough, uneven, full of holes. This made walking difficult, but the planters were accustomed to this sort of thing. There were about twenty of them; they flocked into the long, low wooden shack where hundreds of sable human beings already stood, and at once they began to choose those whom they thought would serve them best, and to demand their price. The captain and his officers, with one or two local men who had

a financial interest in this venture began to haggle. An
auctioneer stood ready to preside over any auction that
might take place. The murmur of voices rose higher and
higher, offers were accepted or refused, protests were voiced,
altercations as to whether credit should be given or cash
paid down took place. A babel soon was the result. But still
the sale went steadily on.

The men and women disposed of were taken out of the
shack and grouped according to their new owners under the
charge of black 'drivers' brought up from the country to
take the new slaves to the several estates to which they would
henceforth belong. Presently there were only thirty or forty
persons left to be sold. Among these was Psyche. 'How much
do you ask for that girl?' enquired Huntingdon of one of the
vendors.

'I think we shall put her and some others up for auction,
Mr. Huntingdon,' said the captain, interposing; 'I shouldn't
be surprised if that girl was a queen in her own country.'

'What difference would that make here?' laughed Huntingdon; 'besides, I fancy you have brought other "queens" to
Jamaica in the past, though these never seemed aware of
their former royalty.'

The captain grinned, some of the assembled planters
laughed out. 'Well, anyhow,' rejoined the captain, 'she's
a fine, strong girl, and young. And very good-looking, too,
me lord. She's worth a lot more than any other woman I
have brought this time. It would surprise you to learn how
much I paid for her in Africa.'

'That too is what you always say, McClintock,' scoffed a
planting attorney; 'and I'm sure we'd be surprised to hear
how little you do pay for the slaves you sell us at such
exorbitant prices. Well, I'll give you fifty pounds for her,
and you know that that's top price for a woman.'

The captain strove to prevent a pleased expression from
stealing over his face, The bidding had begun excellently;
was good even if it got no farther. But he shook his head

deprecatingly, as though he had actually been asked to make Psyche a present to Mr. Simon Jones.

'I'll give you sixty,' said Huntingdon quietly.

'Sixty-five!' This bid came from an old gentleman whose age was the exact figure of his bid. Everybody there knew that if he bought Psyche she would become one of his 'ladies' on some one of his numerous estates. On a conservative estimate he already had about twenty-five of these odalisques, but he seemed not averse from adding to the number.

'Seventy,' cried Jones, who was reflecting that Psyche could both be a pleasant companion and also the mother of many children who would be useful in the future. But Mr. Jones was secretly startled by his own extravagance.

Huntingdon hesitated. He did not wish to appear too anxious to purchase this girl. But she seemed aware that different men were bidding for her, and she kept her eyes on him. Was there a sort of entreaty in them? He scoffed at the idea. What would a savage know of what was going on? Yet, in a way, he was secretly pleased. And he did not like either of his rivals at this auction.

'A hundred pounds,' he said calmly.

Those about him gasped. Seventy pounds had appeared to them a pretty stiff sum to offer for the girl: a hundred was extraordinary. They were puzzled too as to the reason for this bid.

Although no one could know, in days of little communication and bad roads, what took place on a neighbouring estate but a couple of miles away, yet it was generally understood that Huntingdon (astonishingly) did not follow the general custom of the country and keep mistresses. He lived alone in his Great House, he had—so report went—no children. It was whispered that he had not been loathe to leave England for Jamaica because of a bitter disappointment in love; and his restraint both in drinking and in sex affairs was regarded now as something permanent, even while it was sneered at by those of his own calling. Yet here was he, buying a young girl at a wildly extravagant price. What, asked some of those at the auction, could possibly be his reason?

The auctioneer implored the other bidders to go better than Huntingdon; he discovered extraordinary excellencies in Psyche, turning her round and round for all to see, pointing out her unusual features, pinching her jutting breasts. But no further bid was forthcoming. The deal was closed.

Presently the purchases were marched off by the Negro drivers towards places in the city where they would stay for the night, their journey country-wards to begin before day-break next morning. They would walk every foot of the distance, stopping at night at villages or towns which they would reach at nightfall. Psyche noticed that the young man with the straight nose, thin, proud lips and clear blue eyes had spoken last when she was being sold, and felt that he was now her owner. His driver took her by the arm and led her outside. Huntingdon accompanied him.

'Cato,' he said, 'you needn't brand this girl; it's a pity that any of them have to be branded.'

When Psyche emerged from the wharf with her nine companions the scene she observed on either hand and before her was strange and bewildering to her; she had known nothing like it before. The shops in the streets through which the slaves passed in a sort of procession were open now; in the streets themselves gentlemen rode on horses on their way to work, or drove in small carriages drawn by a single horse. Carts crawled along, pulled by mules or oxen, their drivers walking at their side and incessantly cracking the long whips they carried in their hands. Black and yellow women moved about with trays and bundles poised and balanced on their heads crying out wares in a tongue that was new to the young slave girl. Hogs rooted in the heaps of refuse in the streets, dogs fought one another for the bones they had somehow procured, or wandered idly to and fro. The thoroughfares were full of holes and sandy; there were no sidewalks; the passing of this new batch of slaves scarcely drew anything more than a casual glance or a word or two from the people in the streets. All was sordid, and the sun's heat smote everyone with a pitiless impartiality; nevertheless, to Psyche it was all wonderful. She particularly noticed that the women in the streets wore some sort of clothing and were by no means as scantily attired as the slaves. And, had she understood what was said, she would have known that some of these towns-folk, most of whom were bondspeople themselves, now and then scornfully alluded to the newcomers as 'guinea nagers', or as 'guinea birds'.

She and the others turned west after walking upwards for about half a mile, and presently were herded in shacks in large yards piled high here and there with grass. These were the grass-yards of Kingston. There they would stay and rest for that day, and in the morning they would say farewell to Kingston.

Chapter 2

OLD THINGS AND NEW

'You seem to be happy here, Psyche.'

The girl started, surprised to be addressed by her master in her native Mandingo dialect.

'Yes, master,' she replied; 'you treat me well.'

'Tell me something about your life in your own country, Psyche.'

'But how, master, do you understand my language? You have never lived over there?' Psyche pointed in what she believed to be the general direction of Africa; as a matter of fact she was pointing towards the north.

'No; I have never been in Africa; but you must surely know by now that there are many people on this estate who come from your part of that country. I have learnt the tongue from them, and I can speak the Eboe tongue also, and one or two others—not much, you know, but enough to make myself understood.'

Psyche looked with awe upon her young master. She naturally expected that he would know everything, but in this she had never thought to include her own language. She herself was picking up English, slave English now for the most part, but she would talk in the Mandingo dialect to those on the estate who hailed from her own part of the Dark Continent, never dreaming that any white man could comprehend what she said.

She had arrived at Hope Vale, in the parish of St. James, a month before. Huntingdon had remained in Kingston to transact some business, then had gone on to the capital, Spanish Town, where he had stayed a week. The driver who had taken Psyche and the other slaves to Hope Vale had borne a letter from him to the estate's overseer; that letter from Mr. Huntingdon had instructed the man in charge of the estate's working to use Psyche well, not to put her to work in the cane fields but to find for her some household job. She had therefore been installed in the cook-house, as the kitchen was called in those days, under the head cook, a woman of sixty years of age whose son was the driver who had been put in charge of the slaves in Kingston. He had quickly told her of the price Mr. Huntingdon had paid for the girl; this had caused the old woman to regard Psyche with great respect. There was another reason too why she should look upon Psyche as a young woman out of the ordinary. This woman had come from the Mandingo country in early youth. She knew what Psyche meant when the latter had one day informed her, in tones that admitted of no dispute, that 'In my own country I was a priestess'.

It was afternoon; Psyche had been standing a little beyond the cook-house when her master had come upon her suddenly with his question. Her whole body was now clothed in a print cotton dress, as became one of the maids attached to the house, but her feet were bare, and round her ankles her anklets shone brightly. Lithe, tall, with shining eyes, ebony in hue but with the tell-tale nose that spoke of her partly semitic extraction, she was striking to look at in comparison with the other women on the estate, despite the ill-fitting clothing that she wore. And now she could talk at ease, for the language that the master used was her own.

She told him her story. She had grown up with the other girls of her village, planting food, weaving mats, attending to the chores of her hut from morn to eve. Then she had been chosen as a priestess when she was fifteen; at sixteen she was to be married to some man who would pay her father liberally for her. But there had been a war between neighbouring tribes and her own, and her husband to-be had been killed as well as many of the younger men of her village and famine had nearly come, but had been averted just in time by good seasons. So, because she was believed to have directly brought the welcome rain as a priestess, and also because the price her father demanded for her as a wife was higher than the men could afford to pay, it was decided that she should continue as priestess for another year. She knew that this was a rare honour, though not unprecedented.

Then one night the village had been attacked by slave-raiders. She and several others had fled to the surrounding forest, but had been hunted down and caught by the victors. She had been taken to the coast, and there sold to a slave factory, which in turn had disposed of her to Captain McClintock. A simple oft-told tale which almost every West African village could relate.

'A priestess, eh?' commented Mr. Huntingdon humor-ously. 'Then you were a lady of some importance in your own part of the world, Psyche?'

'Yes,' she replied without a moment's hesitation; 'I was very important, master.'

He laughed. 'And you learnt many strange secrets as a priestess?' he enquired.

'Oh, yes, master; I was very powerful.'

She remembered that the evening her village had been attacked she had previously gathered some beans of a plant to dry and crush later on for the doctoring of the spears of those who went out to hunt big game. She had wrapped them up in a piece of pliant kid-skin and had snatched up her tiny parcel when about to flee from the hut. She had concealed them in her hair when she knew she was certain to be caught. All the way from Africa she had treasured and hidden them, not because she thought that they were of any value but because they and the anklets and bangles she wore were her only possessions. Other slaves, she knew, had not even a brass anklet to boast of: nothing except the bush girdle with which they modified their nakedness. But she said nothing about these things now. They seemed utterly unimportant.

'You must have been sorry that your marriage was postponed,' Huntingdon went on, 'or rather, that your intended husband was killed.'

'No, master; I was glad. He was old, though rich, and he had many other wives. Then, perhaps, if I had married him I wouldn't have come here.'

'But here you are a slave, Psyche. How can you possibly like that?'

'I am freer here than I was in my village,' she replied; 'if I had married that old man I would have been his slave too. I like to be here, master—with you.'

'Thanks for the compliment, Psyche. Well, perhaps we shall find you a young husband.'

'You?' she asked.

'Good God, girl, you are very direct! Have you no'—he wanted to say 'modesty,' but could think of no word in her tongue that would express that idea.

'But, master, don't you like me? They say here that you paid a lot of money for me; more'—she continued proudly—'than any master in this country ever paid for a female just come from Africa. Didn't you buy me because you liked me? Why don't you make me one of your wives?'

'I have no "wives", Psyche.'

'Not yet, though you should have, and plenty of children. But I prefer to be the first. I would look after your big hut for you, and prevent people from robbing you, and love you, and give you plenty of children. And I am beautiful, master; everybody says so; they said so in my village when I was little, and I am more beautiful now. I don't want any other husband but you. You will take me, master?'

'This is plain-speaking with a vengeance,' he laughed. 'But I will tell you what I'll do, Psyche, and that will be better for you than taking you as a "wife". I will get the

overseer to give you some shoes, and even stockings if you
like. And you shall have a dress or two that will be smarter
and will fit you better than the one you are wearing now.
I'll see about it to-morrow.'

He laughed again and walked away. She watched him
go with a puzzled frown. He had refused to make her his
own as she had suggested, though ever since the day he had
bought her in Kingston her mind had been set upon that.
There were other men on the estate, white men too, whom
she could have, but none of these did she want. It was he,
and he alone. She loved him. And he was so kind to her . . .
so superior to every other man that she had ever seen. He
was going to give her clothing such as the white women
wore. Better, perhaps, than most of them wore. Then . . .
then. . . . A determined look crept into her face. The blood
of her semitic grandfather stirred within her. She would
not cease to strive for what she wanted.

Charles Huntingdon went into his house, but stood with
a thoughtful air by the open front door, looking out upon
his property as far as eye could reach. Carpets of green
rolled away, green spears of cane topped by soft lilac-
coloured plumes.

The land sloped upwards; where the growing cane
stopped the Negro village of the estate began. Here were
the cottages in which many of the slaves lived with their
families, and about their huts grew coconut palms and
plantain trees; pigs rooted in sties near these habitations,
and babies toddled about. Farther off were barracks for the
men who had no wives on the property; opposite to this
village, and also on rising ground, were the overseer's
house and the estate hospital. To the left were the sugar
works, the mill, the boiling house. These were a scene of
ceaseless activity during all the time when the canes were
reaped and the sugar made. This work would begin next
week.

The master's residence stood upon rising ground also. It

was of but one storey and had been built in the days when slave rebellions were far more feared than now. Its walls of stone were thick and pierced with holes through which the inmates could fire their muskets if attacked; the rooms were unceiled and the heavy rafters showed; these rooms were large but dark, and all round the house ran a veranda sheltered from the sun by jalousie blinds. The furniture was old but solid, nearly all of native mahogany. Huntingdon had changed nothing since he had taken possession. He entertained so little, was so much of a recluse, that he gave no thought to the new style of living and of building which was now rapidly coming into vogue in Jamaica and which had already found expression in such mansions as Rosehall, which was situated not far away on the sea-coast of St. James.

The next morning he rode over to the overseer's house. He had not forgotten his promise to Psyche. For her he ordered three new dresses, a couple of pairs of shoes, and, actually, half a dozen pairs of stockings. It amused him to think how she would look in these, and whether she would not hate to walk about in shoes to which, during all the days of her life, she had been totally unaccustomed.

The overseer received Mr. Huntingdon's orders without raising an eyebrow or asking a question. But when the master had ridden away he sought out his wife—for, though this was unusual, he was a married man—and told her what was afoot.

'I thought it was something like that,' she drawled in her Jamaica accent when he had finished his tale; 'that's why he pay so much for her.'

Mrs. Buxton was a woman of thirty-five, plain, and already much too stout. She was of tradespeople class and born in Jamaica, and always she remembered she was white. Yet she had never dared to think that an overseer or his wife could enter the owner's house as an equal, and she had been secretly glad that Mr. Huntingdon had remained a bachelor. Now, however, she argued, his domestic relations were about to change. Happily (from her point of view) he did not contemplate marriage. To keep a slave girl as a mistress would be entirely a different thing from bringing a white woman and a lady as a wife to the Great House of Hope Vale. That, of course, would have demoted Mrs. Buxton from her proud position of being the only married white woman on this flourishing estate. But she did not quite approve of what she believed to be Mr. Huntingdon's present choice.

'I am not so sure as you are about Psyche,' her husband commented. 'Mr. Huntingdon does some funny things at times. He felt sorry for this girl, I think; but I don't believe he wants her as a "housekeeper".'

His wife sniffed contemptuously. 'You must be blind,' she retorted. 'He may not know his own mind now, but *she* will soon teach him what it is. Shoes and stockings for a nigger gal! And a hundred pounds to buy her! What you think it can mean?'

Buxton shrugged his shoulders thoughtfully. 'You may be right,' he conceded; 'she's rather good-looking.'

'So you've been looking at her, eh? You said the same thing about that other girl who was here two years ago, and who quite suddenly bought her freedom. Where did she get the money from, Thomas, if not from you? I wish you would tell me that!'

Her voice had grown angry; Mr. Buxton thought it was about time for him to hurry to the fields. He regretted that he had mentioned Mr. Huntingdon's order to his better half.

But that same day he sent a man on horseback to Montego Bay for the things which Mr. Huntingdon had commanded him to obtain for Psyche. That afternoon he was able to hand them over to the slave girl; and if the dresses did not fit as well as they might, were really secondhand and intended for the evening wear of ladies, and if the shoes—the size of which he had calculated—were a trifle too large, and the stockings tight, Psyche was not troubled by all this. She had to take off her anklets to wear the stockings. She put them away, and this was like saying goodbye to a part of her former life. She knew she would never wear them again.

Chapter 3

ACCOMPLISHMENT

THE Jamaica dinner hour was four or five o'clock as might be convenient; Mr. Huntingdon preferred to dine at seven.

He dined alone in the dim room with the huge mahogany dining-table, the great sideboards on which polished silver gleamed, amidst the chairs all made of mahogany, seats and everything, the air coming through windows with stone embrasures two feet thick, which were shuttered at night, for the windows were not glazed. The floor was innocent of any sort of carpeting, but highly polished and dark; a chandelier hung from a beam overhead but the table was lighted by candles set in silver sconces. And always there were at least four servants to wait upon him, though he often thought that one would have sufficed.

This evening the cook had prepared a special feast, as though he had returned after months of absence from his home. He ate but little, however, feeling moody and restless. He made it a rule to take coffee after dinner, and this was always served by a man servant; he now sat waiting for it and presently received a surprise.

For coffee was brought in by Psyche walking slowly and with great care; Huntingdon would have laughed but that he instinctively realised that that might have hurt the girl's feelings. He saw at once that her careful, precarious gait was the consequence of the shoes she now wore for the first time in her life; she walked in fear and trembling lest she should pitch headlong to the floor as the result of one false step.

She was dressed in something made of flowered silk, cut low; an evening dress originally that she had been given that afternoon. Her skirt spread out in flounces; her arms were bare. She held out the tray of silver as far from her body as she could, placed it on the table, and then looked at him enquiringly. She was clearly at a loss as to what she should do next.

'So you are butlering tonight, eh?' he asked kindly, talking in her own dialect. 'How did you come to get this job?'

'I asked the cook, master, to let me do this; I told her you wanted it.'

'But I don't remember saying anything of the kind, Psyche,' he replied, as he placed a cup before him and reached out for the coffee-pot, she watching intently to see just what he would do.

'You didn't, master, but I mightn't have been allowed to come to you unless I had said that you wanted me to.'

'Do you know the difference between truth and falsehood, Psyche?' he asked, as, anticipating his wishes, she handed him the milk jug.

She nodded affirmatively, then said: 'But it is true that you prefer me to the man who brings in your coffee.'

'Well, I dare say it is,' he agreed, 'now that you are here; but it won't do, you know, for you to use my name as an authority for your own premeditated acts.'

'You can always tell me afterwards if I displease you,' she answered, 'and then I won't do again what you object to.'

'My good girl!' he exclaimed, 'what do you imagine you are?'

'Your housekeeper,' she said calmly.

She had heard that word since she had been at Hope Vale; she had been told that all unmarried white men, and married ones also, and many who were not white, sported 'housekeepers', that that was a regular custom, and that her young master was considered a peculiar and inexplicable exception. He lived alone, and had always done so. But rumour on Hope Vale said that Psyche had been bought to fill the position vacant for so many years. And she herself wanted and was planning that it should be so. She had tried to interest him in her viewpoint the day before; she was trying again. And now she was inside the house with him, her story that he had willed it so having been accepted without question by the cook.

'I wish no housekeeper, Psyche; I hinted that to you only yesterday afternoon,' he replied in tones of finality.

She looked at him steadily; his eyes were on his cup. She answered nothing.

When he had finished coffee she went to the sideboard and brought to him a decanter of madeira and a large wineglass. She silently filled the glass, though she had been told often that Mr. Huntingdon drank no liquor either at dinner or after.

Mechanically he took up the glass and began to sip its contents; she filled it again when it was empty, but he shook his head.

'I think I have had enough,' he said.

'You are tired, master; you came home only yesterday; this will do you no harm.'

'Well, you take a glass, too, Psyche, if you think so much of it.'

She had sampled the stuff before surreptitiously, just a little at a time, since she had been about the house. She knew how potent it was, how it went to one's head and made one bold and reckless. So she poured out for herself but half a glass, yet when her master had emptied his she again filled it up. He did not remonstrate this time or even hesitate. He tossed it off. He felt less melancholy, indeed he had become exhilarated. 'Sit down,' he said to her, 'and we shall talk more comfortably. Do you know that you are wearing a white woman's clothes?'

'Yes,' she answered, 'and I want to be a white woman.'

'Good Lord! is there anything more that you desire?'

She looked puzzled, not understanding what he meant.

'Drink your wine and sit down,' he again ordered, at the same time refilling his own glass. Her eyes gleamed with pleasure as she heard him. The distance between them seemed perceptibly diminished.

'So you want to be white, is that it?' he continued, looking at her with a smile.

'No master, for I can't be white in colour. But I want to be a white woman.'

He laughed. 'Please explain,' he suggested.

The wine she had taken was affecting her now. It loosened her tongue completely. 'I mean,' she said in a forthright fashion, 'that I want to dress like I am now, and to wear shoes always, though they hurt. And I want to live in this house and look after you and it, and have slaves under me, like the wife of your headman'—by which word she meant Mr. Huntingdon's overseer. 'And then when we have children they too will be white, and they will grow up and be like you.'

He smiled sadly; she noticed this and misunderstood what was passing in his mind.

She became eager: 'I am young, I can have plenty of children, master: why do you doubt that?'

'And that's your idea of bestowing blessings, eh? You seem to be always harping on children. Do you understand that if you had children they would be slaves? Would you like that?'

'They wouldn't be slaves,' she answered with placid assurance, then poured herself out another half-glass of madeira. He filled his own glass once more.

'Let me tell you something, Psyche,' he said. 'I have an elder brother in England; he is a big chief there. Do you understand?'

'Yes.'

'And he, though very lucky, may die before me: and as yet he has no children. Now, if he died I should have to go from Jamaica and become the big chief in his place. Do you understand?'

She nodded affirmatively.

'But you and your "plenty of children", if you had them, could never go with me. Have you thought of that?'

She had not, but the matter seemed to her of no importance whatever. Why should he wish to tell her all this?

'And when I die, if my brother should then be alive, or he should by then have any children, even this property would be theirs. That is the law, you know. I could not leave it to your children.'

She stared at him blankly. What on earth did all this mean? What strange palaver it was!

Others would have thought so too, white as well as black. White men would have laughed to hear Huntingdon talk all this stuff. They would have been scandalised that he should have spoken to the girl as if she were an equal, or even white. And what would she care about the possibilities of the future, anyhow? After all, she was only a slave.

'I have lived a lonely life in this country,' he went on, communing with himself more than with her; but he still spoke in the Mandingo dialect, and she followed him. 'I have kept myself aloof from others, white or black or brown. And now . . .'

He continued musing, silently she again filled his glass, and then she gathered up the things on the table, leaving only the decanter. He did not seem to see her go, but sat there for another hour, thinking on his past fortunes and his prospects.

Mechanically he had continued to drink. Never before, since he had been in Jamaica, had he drunk so much. At last he rose and went towards his room. His earlier feeling of exhilaration had passed; he did not realise that it had been replaced by a spirit of recklesness, nor did he imagine that this was what Psyche had hoped for, that this was why she had placed the wine before him.

His bedroom was lighted by candles which shed a dim light upon high canopied bed and huge chairs. At a glance he saw her. She had thrown off her dress; she was standing, waiting for him with but a single garment on; as he entered she quickly blew out two of the three lighted tapers. She did not speak a word.

When at length the dawn came he said: 'They will be wondering outside what has become of you, Psyche.'

'No,' she answered simply, 'I told them yesterday that in the night I would be with you.'

Chapter 4

THE NET IS SPREAD

Mrs. Buxton, the wife of the Overseer of Hope Vale, was permanently displeased. Mr. Huntingdon had at last taken to himself a housekeeper, which was right and proper in its way, according to the custom of the country. But instead of setting up some nice-looking free brown female at the Great House he had chosen this slave girl who had come but the other day to Jamaica. It is true that this had been expected, but now that it had happened Mrs. Buxton felt outraged. The young woman simply did not know her place. She gave herself airs and ruled it with a high hand, and no one dared complain to Mr. Huntingdon about her.

Mrs. Buxton, assured in her position as the one white woman on the estate, had spoken to Psyche one day about some household arrangement—she, a white woman and a married woman to boot, had condescended to do this. And the impertinent thing had actually, almost, told her to mind her own business. Flesh and blood could not stand this, and yet Mrs. Buxton's flesh and blood had continued to stand it since there was nothing else to be done. But some day, she thought grimly, she would get even with 'this nigger gal'. An opportunity would assuredly present itself.

'And now he drinks too,' muttered Mr. Buxton angrily, talking to his wife. 'He never did that before.'

Mr. Buxton would not have minded if Charles Huntingdon had taken heavily to drink from the day he set foot at Hope Vale, for in that case there might have been more opportunities for a certain Mr. Buxton to feather his nest properly under the very nose of his employer. But now that

Huntingdon drank as he had never done before, he had by his side a young woman who, instead of remembering what she was, and contenting herself with being but a sort of upper servant in the Great House, went about looking into estate affairs in general. Though she could not understand them she seemed to see to it that Huntingdon kept his attention fixed on them; also, she encouraged some of the more intelligent slaves to talk to her and tell her what was going on. This information she imparted to her master, while at the same time she gradually tightened her hold upon all that concerned the Great House, and directed the other domestics as though they were her property. One or two who had been long on the estate started to rebel. They objected to Psyche's assumption of authority. But they too discovered, like Mr. Buxton, that there was nothing to be gained by taking complaints to Mr. Huntingdon. Indeed, as a result of such complaints, Psyche had had a couple of them summarily removed from the position of domestic servants and sent once more to labour in the fields.

She now always waited on her master herself, never allowing the other slaves to do so. It was usually while functioning as butleress that she retailed to him all the news she had picked up, during the week or day, or had caused to be gathered for her, and if some of it was lies and pure malice, some was true and of value. For nearly a year now she had been 'housekeeper', and she had thought that by this time she would have had a child. But there was not the slightest sign of one. This angered her. She wondered whether any of the folk on the estate had bewitched her or something, and particularly she thought of Mrs. Buxton. She knew that Mrs. Buxton hated her. She also hated that lady, and, if she could, would have implemented her hatred with murder.

With Mr. and Mrs. Buxton was sitting this morning a girl who had come over from a neighbouring estate, Plimsole, to spend a few days with them. She was the daughter of the head carpenter of Plimsole, lived but two miles away as the road went, was now nearly twenty years of age, and undeniably pretty. Josephine had actually been twice engaged, but both her intendeds had very quickly broken off the engagement. For her temper was fiery, and she had shown it only too plainly to men who shuddered with horror at the thought of having to live until death with such a bitter-tongued woman.

That had been a lesson to her. Latterly she had endeavoured to keep her temper more in check when dealing with persons of her own colour.

'Mr. Huntingdon is handsome,' she now broke into the conversation; 'I have seen him twice since I have been here; twice yesterday.' She spoke with the drawl of the poorly educated Jamaica white woman of the middle class. Her complexion had not been affected by the sun, and her long golden hair and keen blue eyes bespoke her Nordic inheritance. There was, however, something rather common about her. Her look and gestures proclaimed her plebeian origin and the tendencies of her disposition.

'And he didn't even give you a glance, I am sure,' commented Mrs. Buxton wrathfully, 'he has eyes only for his nigger gal.'

'Oh, I don't know. Perhaps he did.'

'Well, he wouldn't marry anyone in our station,' murmured Mr. Buxton, 'so there's no use your thinking of him, Jose. We don't count in his sight.'

'He's taught this nigger gal of his to talk like himself,' said Mrs. Buxton, 'instead of like a nigger. You should hear her clipping up! Yet, when she came here, she could only talk some damn African language. I never see anything like this before!'

'She don't mix with the other slaves?' asked Josephine incredulously. 'What she think she is?'

'A lady, I suppose; a black lady,' replied Mrs Buxton with heavy sarcasm. 'She actually wears shoes, like white people! It's a joke!'

Mr. Buxton rose to go, his 'second breakfast' over. He agreed with all his wife had said, but it was not wise for an overseer to indulge in or to listen to much caustic criticism of his employer or of his employer's favourites. Chance remarks had a way of coming to ears for which they had not been intended.

The two women, left alone, continued their conversation. They spoke confidentially.

'I couldn't expect him to marry me,' said Josephine, in a low reflective tone of voice, as though she were thinking out something, 'but I would like to take him away from that black slave girl.'

'I wish you could, Jose,' eagerly agreed Mrs. Buxton; 'but you can't. He is too wrapped up with her. Besides, *you* couldn't be his "housekeeper" here. You are white, and you must either marry, or remain an old maid, or——' The lady paused, not knowing whether or not she should be more explicit.

'Well, with a man like Huntingdon, wouldn't that be better than marrying some man who don't have much?' enquired Josephine quietly. 'So long,' she added, 'as it wasn't too open?'

Mrs. Buxton's eyes gleamed. 'You could live in Montego Bay, if you liked,' she commented, 'and he could come there at night time to see you. It isn't far. But you would have to get him first, and you would have to make him give up this girl. I don't see how you're going to do that.'

'He would do it if he loved me,' answered Josephine confidently, 'an' he can't possibly love a nigger. She is only a convenience.'

'But how you going to meet him?' enquired Mrs. Buxton, fired now with the idea of seeing Psyche driven to take her place as an ordinary slave on the estate and subject to her orders. 'He wouldn't come here if I asked him; an' I wouldn't fit to ask him. And that black imp of hell would know.'

'He was riding by the river when I was going to bathe yesterday,' said Josephine suddenly. 'He often go that way?'

'Every day, at about half-past twelve o'clock, when he going to the Great House.'

'Then I am going there now,' said Josephine with decision. She sprang up and hurried off for a towel without saying another word. Mrs. Buxton eyed her doubtfully, wondering what was in her mind. Whatever it was, thought the lady, it was bound to fail. Mr. Huntingdon had eyes for none except 'his nigger gal'.

There was a riding path by the river, which was screened in some places by rows of trees growing on its banks. Behind some of these trees, and at a spot below where water for drinking purposes was baled out of the flowing stream, the white people on the estate sometimes bathed; should anyone pass by, it was easy enough for the bather to hide his or her body for a while; for this reason, perhaps, the trees were never disturbed.

Josephine now hurried to this spot, which was but about a furlong from Mr. Buxton's house. She disrobed entirely, then slipped silently into the water at its deepest part thereabouts. Her plan was simple, even primitive. She had not long to wait before the sound of a horse's hooves on the river bank came to her ears; the rider could surely be none else than Mr. Huntingdon. When he was almost abreast of her, she commenced to scream. Naturally, he pulled in his horse, sprang off, and hurried to the river's edge. In front of him was a white girl, half submerged, who yelled out that she was drowning and seemed to be struggling to extricate herself from something: she was not looking in his direction. He didn't see how she could possibly be in danger, as the river was nowhere so deep that one could not stand upright in it with one's chest well above its surface; it ran, besides, with but ordinary velocity. This woman was evidently a stranger, and apparently had given way to unnecessary fright. But he must reassure her. She was quite obviously white, and it would never do for any male slave, hearing her voice, to come upon her all unclothed as she now was.

'You are all right,' he called out to her; 'you can easily walk to the bank.'

'Oh,' she gasped, 'I didn't know. It is deep here, and my foot has caught in some rushes or something.' Which was true in a way, as she had deliberately wound her foot among the tall rushes that grew here and there in the river bed.

'You are only frightened,' he replied. 'Pull out your foot and wade ashore.''

She obeyed instantly, and, seemingly because she was still frightened, made no ado about his seeing her all nude. He held out his hand to her and she clambered up the bank. Then she sank down as though she were exhausted, while he walked to where her clothes lay and brought them to her.

She hastily covered her body, as if for the first time aware that she was naked. 'Thank you,' she drawled, 'I might have drowned if you hadn't come along.'

'Not a chance,' he assured her. 'You haven't bathed here before, have you?'

'No, sir; I came to stay with Mrs. Buxton only yesterday. I am Josephine Brookfield from Plimsole.'

'Well, tell Mrs. Buxton from me that, when next a pretty girl comes to stay with her, she should tell her about this place. If you are all right now, I'll be going, Josephine.'

'Couldn't you stop a minute behind those trees, Mr. Huntingdon, till I get dressed, and then show me the way to Mr. Buxton's house?'

'But surely you must know it? Why . . .'

'Then you can't stay even a minute or two?'

'Well, certainly, if that will help you. You say you are from Plimsole, don't you?'

'Yes sir'—she had almost said 'Massa,' but caught herself up just in time. She must not talk to him as she so often did at home.

She knew that she was excellently formed, that no one in the parish had shoulders and breasts which were more beautiful than hers. And if there was already a certain hardness about her face, he did not notice it, nor had he observed that her hair, in spite of her pretended fight, had not been touched by water or been in any way disturbed. Her full lips were smiling at him, even as she fingered her dress as though to conceal her nudity. Then he turned his back and walked away, and in a few minutes she was clothed and calling out to him. The first part of her plan had succeeded.

They walked together to Buxton's house, the horse following behind. 'Won't you come in an' have a drink, sir?' she asked, smiling brightly at him. He hesitated a moment, then accepted her invitation. Mrs. Buxton, all curtsies, was thunderstruck to see him in her house. This was the first time he had crossed its threshold. She wondered how this miracle had been accomplished by Josephine.

He took a glass of wine, then held out his hand to say goodbye.

'Till we meet again?' the girl enquired.

'But you're leaving here tomorrow, aren't you? I seem to have heard so. Someone told me, I remember now, that you were coming here for a day or two.' He did not mention that his informant had been Psyche; but Mrs. Buxton and Josephine guessed it.

'Yes, but I live at Plimsole, only two miles away,' replied the younger woman. 'Of course my father is only a carpenter, but I would like to see you again.' She beseeched him with her eyes. Too much modesty, or pretence at such, would not suit her purpose now.

'Well, some time I may drop over at Plimsole,' he promised, 'though I don't leave Hope Vale much.'

'I'm giving a party this week,' she said—that was her determination of the moment—'to a few. Of course, my friends are all ordinary people, and you are a big buckra;

but as you are not married that shouldn't matter. Will you come?'

'When is this party?'

'Saturday night.'

'Very well, I'll be there, Josephine. Thank you for your invitation.'

He went then, and did not notice that the servant who had brought in the wine had been carefully listening to his conversation. Nor would he have thought anything of it had he done so. Certainly Mrs. Buxton did not, nor Josephine: what had they to hide from a slave? But the girl told someone else all she had heard, and this included Jose's recital to Mrs. Buxton as to how Mr. Huntingdon had come upon her naked in the river. And that evening Psyche was told the whole tale. Psyche felt that she wanted to know more about Miss Josephine Brookfield.

Chapter 5

A VISIT TO PLIMSOLE

MR. BUXTON was not a good judge of the finer shades, the more delicate nuances, of character or behaviour; yet he could not but perceive that Mr. Huntingdon had altered much in the last year or so, and he was right in attributing this change to the influence of Psyche. Charles Huntingdon himself felt that he had badly broken down under the pressure of conditions. True, he was now doing only what everybody else in the island did, and doing it but moderately, but even that fall from his own previous level of conduct meant much more to him than Psyche would ever be able to realise. Not that it would have made any difference to her procedure had she realised it; she cared for her master, but she did not wish him to remain aloof from her and she could see in his new mode of life nothing whatever for him to regret. He was now, in her view, merely normal, and that was right.

But now he had met this girl, Josephine Brookfield, and she had shown plainly enough that he had greatly attracted her. Coming to think over the episode of the river, he arrived at the conclusion that she had never imagined that she was in any danger whatever, but had simply wished to compel his attention. He was amused. A year before he would have been disgusted.

He was not an expansive person; he did not talk about himself and his feelings to others. He was still lonely in spite of the companionship of his 'housekeeper', and this companionship was, after all, erected on a basis of physical attraction only. Psyche was black, and a savage still at heart; he was white and a cultivated man. Besides, the two

were entirely different races. The only girl of his own race
whom he had met of late was this Josephine Brookfield, and
he was conscious every hour since he had seen her of her
undeniable bodily perfections. Well, he would go to her
party; he would no longer hold himself apart from the life
of Jamaica. There were no critics to condemn him. On the
estates each owner or attorney was a law unto himself in so
far as his personal conduct was concerned.

Early on Friday morning Psyche, who now knew parts
of the parish very well, left Hope Vale, having given out
that she was going into the town of Montego Bay. She rode
one of the estate's horses; when she went fairly long distances
she usually chose this mode of transportation. Mrs.
Buxton was always outraged at this: only white people
should ride, was her firm conviction, and the white man or
woman who could not afford a horse was 'poor buckra for
true'. But that a black girl should ride anywhere was a
defiance of the laws of nature. Regardless of Mrs Buxton's
feelings, however, Psyche continued to defy the laws of
nature. So, this Friday morning, she went off upon a horse.

But she did not take the way to Montego Bay. Instead,
she went in the opposite direction, to Plimsole, riding along
the road that bordered the beach of the bay where lay the
tiny wooden piers from which were shipped the sugar and
rum manufactured by the neighbouring estates.

When she reached the spot from which opened one of the
easy back entrances into Plimsole (for she did not dare ride
through the main entrance), she glimpsed across the water
the roofs of Montego Bay. The town looked diminutive from
this viewpoint. On the hills that rose behind and to the
east of it were the larger planters' houses, like castles
dominating the homes and businesses of those who depended
for security on the lords who lived above. Save for the town
and Great Houses, the scene before her eyes was one of
green and silver: green woods and fields of cane, silver sea
that glinted and shimmered in the still early sun of the

morning. And over all brooded an atmosphere of quiet and of peace. But Psyche gave no thought to the beauty about her, never saw it. She turned her horse, climbed the rise that divided the estate of Plimsole from the road, and found herself in the estate.

Her advent occasioned surprise. A black girl on a horse was an event, something unprecedented. What had she come for, who could she be? To whom could she possibly have brought a message—for surely she must be on an errand for someone. The slaves glanced at her curiously; a headman hailed her, asked her business. She replied that she had come to see a man, a slave from her own country who had arrived in Jamaica on the ship with her a year ago. She believed that, as he was old, he was attached to the household of Mr. Brookfield. Could anyone direct her to Mr. Brookfield's house?

'Dere is de house,' replied the headman, pointing to a single-storey wooden building not far away, 'but you better git off dat 'orse an' walk. Nagars don't ride here. De young missis would hab a fit if she eber see y'u.'

'I will leave the horse here,' she agreed, dismounting, and tying the reins to a branch of a nearby tree. 'Give him an eye for me, please.'

The Negro slave driver noticed her accent, her manner of speaking, perceived her self-assurance, observed her independent air. 'Massa me Gawd!' he exclaimed. 'Dis is de firs' time me eber see black gal talk an' walk an' ride like white.' He shook his head wonderingly as if this was a problem quite beyond him. But Psyche was already on her way to the carpenter's house, and did not so much as give the headman another thought.

Skilled carpenters were paid more than the overseers on these self-contained properties; so Josephine's father lived pretty comfortably for those times, and, his wife being dead, and Jose not tolerating anything like a 'housekeeper' within the paternal home—housekeepers could be maintained outside quite easily—she was the boss of this establishment. Round to the back of it walked Psyche, and there luck favouring her, she found the old man, the gigantic Negro who had come to Jamaica with her. He was a general servant attached to the house except when the cane crop commenced, when he would help reap the cane in the fields like the others. He had been a headman, a sort of Elder Statesman, in Psyche's village but eighteen months before, when she had been a priestess; now he was only a slave. She had known for some time that he lived on Plimsole, but this was the first occasion they had seen one another since they had parted many months ago in Kingston. He stared at her, astonished. She wore the dress of the white women, her feet were shod with shoes, her head was protected from the sun by a tasteful turban. Surely it must be her magic that had won her these things. But he was shrewd. Almost instantly he guessed that her talisman had been her good looks; knew that she must now be some great buckra's mistress. Yet her magic may have helped her to this position too.

'Mashimba,' said she rapidly, speaking to him in their common native tongue, 'I hear there's to be a party here tomorrow night. I want you to help me come to it.'

'A black girl at a white party?' he gasped. 'Do you know what you are saying?'

She gestured impatiently. 'I only want to watch it from outside; from the yard. You can find me a good place, and explain to any people who may see me that I have come here to see you. Say I am your daughter or niece and that I live near here. Don't tell them I am from Hope Vale.'

'They will find that out in good time,' he answered positively; 'but you can come tomorrow night, only I shall be very busy. Lots of slaves go from estate to estate after nightfall to visit their loves. Why do you want to come?'

'To see this party. Also'—for she knew she could trust him, and of a sudden resolved to be candid—'also, my white

man is invited to the party, and I want to see whom he
meets and what happens. Can you help me?'

'Who invited him?' asked Mashimba.

'The white girl, Josephine Brookfield.'

'Phew. She wants to take him away, take him for herself?'

'Perhaps. But she won't.'

'She will; but of course he may still keep you. You are his
slave, so. . . .'

'I will know what she wants to do tomorrow night. Then
I will know too what I want to do. I am a priestess,
remember, Mashimba.'

She spoke more confidently than she felt, but she had to
impress this man. She succeeded too, for he became more
deferential than before. 'I will arrange that you shall see
the party,' he agreed, 'everybody else here who wants to see
it can do so; there is nothing to prevent them. Come here at
about nine o'clock; other strangers will be here, so no one
will notice you particularly; but now I——' He started, and
the remainder of the sentence was unuttered. For at that
moment Josephine appeared on the upper tread of the
short flight of wooden steps leading to the ground. She saw
the two talking together. Idling. And not disguising that
fact even. She called out sharply: 'Who is that, Homer?'—
the name borne by the African in his new home—'and
what is that girl doing away from her work?'

Mashimba stammered something unintelligible; Josephine stared more sharply at the girl. 'Oh!' she exclaimed
as recognition came to her, 'it is that slut from Hope Vale.
Well, what she doing here?'

'I came to see my old relative, missis,' responded Psyche
respectfully, knowing that, if possible, she must avoid
angering Josephine.

'You have no right to: you should be cleaning cane in the
fields. Did you ask Mrs. Buxton if you could come?'

Josephine knew that Mrs. Buxton had no kind of juris-
diction over Psyche, but deliberately chose to forget that. She

was glad of this opportunity of openly humiliating Psyche.

'Well, why don't you answer me?' she demanded shrilly, as Psyche racked her brain to find a suitable reply.

'I am going to Montego Bay, missis, but thought I would call here for a little while.'

'Montego Bay is the other way round, and you know it, you black liar. You ought to be flogged. I think I will tell your master so; that will teach you not to wander about enticing men and keeping other people's slaves from their business. Homer, go right on with your work!'

'Yes, missis,' muttered the man humbly, and hurried off without another word, leaving Psyche to bear alone the brunt of the young woman's anger.

Josephine came slowly down the steps and walked up to Psyche with a glint of contempt and anger in her eye. She wished that Psyche would utter one impertinent word; she even hoped that the girl, forgetting herself completely, would make some show of physical violence. For that, though Psyche did not belong to this estate, would have been an unpardonable crime, to be punished with flogging and imprisonment; while impertinence would meet with summary and by no means gentle ejection at the hands of robust male slaves. Somehow, Psyche read Josephine's wishes and intentions in her looks, and kept a stern grip upon herself. This was not Hope Vale. And her master was not on the spot.

'Sorry, missis,' she forced herself to say: 'I beg pardon.'

'Well, I don't want any idle sluts round here, you understand,' rapped out Josephine. 'Very likely you come here to try to steal something—all of you t'ief. And you are dressed up too! You look like a Christmas poppy-show. I don't think I ever see a blacker slut than you in me life, or a uglier. What part of Africa you come from?'

Psyche did not answer; she turned to leave.

'Answer me at once,' snapped Josephine; 'I don't put up with any nonsense from poppy-show slave gals.'

But Psyche, knowing that she had done nothing to merit punishment, and that she could not be detained against her will, went on her way, followed by the scornful laughter of Josephine. 'You may be the housekeeper of Mr. Huntingdon now,' volleyed that young lady after her; 'but you won't be for long, I can tell you. You going to dig canehole before many weeks, and I will come to see you do it. Fancy walking into Plimsole in broad daylight as you like! I never hear of such a piece of forwardness from a nigger slut before. Next time I will set me dogs on you! Now clear out here!'

But by this Psyche was making rapid progress towards her horse, keeping her lips tightly shut, realising that Josephine knew all about her and never doubting that Josephine would work hard to see her flung down among the field labourers as soon as possible. Yet even when she was out of Plimsole and on her way to the town of Montego Bay she did not burst into tears, or rave, or curse. That was not her habit or in accordance with her character. She was thinking swiftly; a war had been declared between her and this white lady, with all the weapons in the hands of the white lady. She was beautiful: Psyche frankly faced that fact. She was Mr. Huntingdon's own colour. She had made up her mind to have Mr. Huntingdon; that river scene was sufficient proof of that; and now there was this open and unwarranted abuse. And she, Psyche, had not even a child by which she might retain some hold upon Charles Huntingdon's affections! Compared with Josephine Brookfield she had nothing, was nothing. Oh, if she only had a child!

Chapter 6

JOSEPHINE WINS

'I MAY not be back before daybreak, Psyche,' said Mr. Huntingdon, 'so you must not wait up for me.'

'Yes, Squire,' answered Psyche, addressing him as the white men did on the estate: he preferred 'squire' to 'master' from her, anyhow.

She saw him ride off; it was then about nine o'clock, and the night was dark save for the stars above.

Hardly had he gone than she slipped into the room which she had been given by special favour when she came to Hope Vale, though now she rarely used it. In a trice she was clothed in rough osnaburg garments such as the slaves wore, and which she had procured some time before, though with no definite reason. She took off her shoes, feeling glad that she had only worn them when in the house and in the squire's presence; they clogged her movements and hurt her feet as a rule. By going barefoot whenever she could, the soles of her feet had retained their original callosity more or less. She could therefore still make good progress bare-footed and this she proposed to do tonight.

With her slave's dress, bare legs, and her head swathed in a multicoloured turban of cotton cloth, she would not be easily recognised in the darkness; as to the journey before her, she could make it by short cuts and be at Plimsole not long after a horse that went at easy pace. Quietly she locked up the Great House and cautiously made her way outside. No one saw her, and the dogs on the property knew her too well to bark.

When she arrived at the neighbouring estate she mingled with the crowd of sightseers who thronged the open yard of

47

Mr. Brookfield's house. To peer in at any festivity in a white man's residence was the privilege of any slave, and if some of these spectators were strangers from neighbouring properties, no one dreamt of denying them a share in this privilege. This was a freedom long established by custom.

Mingled with the other observers, then, she crept close up to a window and peered inside, knowing that she, being enshrouded by darkness, and in the midst of other people, would not be noticed. There were only nine persons within; these were seated round a table which was loaded with a huge variety of foods, fish and vegetable, and with numerous bottles containing madeira and also with jugs of rum punch. There were four women and five men, and none of the women had looks to boast of; hence Josephine queened it consciously among them, seated at the head of the huge table with Mr. Huntingdon to her right. The five men, one of whom was Josephine's father, had for some time been self-conscious and ill at ease; they had not known until his appearance that Squire Huntingdon would be there. Probably, had they known, sheer diffidence and a feeling of inferiority would have prevented them from attending the function. Josephine had guessed that; hence her secrecy. She now enjoyed the triumph of having at her table a real gentleman whose presence would have honoured any dining-room in the parish of St. James. She had introduced Mr. Huntingdon to the rest of her guests as though he were her property. And that, indeed, was the impression she desired to create.

They had sat down to supper at about ten o'clock, and Josephine, knowing that wine could break down the barriers of class for a time if enough of it were taken, had her butlers pass round bottles and jugs unremittingly, while the people at table, with the exception of Huntingdon and herself, proceeded to gorge. Soon the wine and the rum commenced to have their intended effect. The men were talking loudly when Psyche arrived at about eleven o'clock, while more than one of the women, filled to repletion, had pushed their chairs a little away from the table and hoisted their legs thereon.

Laughter and noise of a drunken description filled the room as the hour drew on to midnight; two of the younger men, careless or oblivious of Mr. Huntingdon's presence now, had thrown their arms round the shoulders of the women next to them and were fondling these without any regard for appearances whatever. These young women seemed not to care a jot, but squealed and shouted when the men went too far, and talked in the slave-English that they used at home, and larded their speech with words which in their sober moments they would themselves have declared to be obscene. Josephine's father had passed out, his head resting on the table helplessly. All this Psyche saw and heard from her vantage point by the window, and she was not surprised when Josephine deliberately threw her arm round Charles Huntingdon's neck. Then Josephine leaned against him and whispered something in his ear. They rose from the table quietly, no one paying any attention to them. Josephine led the way out of the house.

The slaves saw them, of course, but merely made way for them. What slaves might think mattered nothing.

The change of atmosphere was grateful to Charles; he stood in the yard and breathed in the cool night air gladly. The candles, the smoke from the men's cigars, the heat from nine or ten ill-bathed waiters—slaves whom Josephine had borrowed for the night of festivity—had made the dining-room close and smelly; it was a pleasant relief to be outside. 'Let's go for a walk,' suggested Josephine in what she imagined to be a whisper. But she spoke loudly, for she too, though she had been careful, had been drinking more than she was accustomed to do.

Psyche was not far from the couple when they came down the steps and set off in the direction that Josephine indicated. They went arm in arm. She slipped from the spectators among whom she had been standing and crept after them, being guided by the sound of their feet as they walked heavily on the hardened earth. Barefooted as she was, and extremely careful, her footsteps could not fall upon their ears.

The front of the head carpenter's house faced the Negro village of Plimsole: it stood upon a slight eminence, as did the other residences of the white men employed on this estate. Through the farms, or canepieces as they were called (which on two sides came close to the house), ran long paths or avenues from twelve to fifteen feet wide, these allowing the workers to cut down the ripened cane easily when croptime came, and enabling ox-wagons and mule-carts to pass to and fro collecting the cane for conveyance to the sugar mill. It was along one of these paths that Josephine led Charles Huntingdon. And as they walked she talked gaily and laughed, pausing in her stride now and then. At these pauses Psyche, listening intently, heard the sound of kisses.

She would not have minded much if the woman kissed had been a slave girl like herself. That a man should have more than one wife she had always taken for granted, had expected indeed that Mr. Huntingdon himself would some day follow a course which she deemed quite natural, inevitable, and which the women of her own country openly approved of since it lessened their incessant toil. But Psyche knew that there could be no place for her if Josephine once established herself in his heart. Josephine hated her, would never cease working against her until she was turned out of the Great House, and would have as an active ally Mrs. Buxton, whose eyes ever disclosed her rooted aversion to Psyche. And now Josephine was taking the squire some-where—she had no doubt as to Josephine's purpose. Hiding in the darkness she followed the two with dogged pertinacity.

The screeching and clamour within the house soon became dulled; Psyche, with eyes attuned to the dense darkness of the narrow avenue (to one side of which she

clung as she slunk along) perceived now a great silk cotton
tree towering up into the skies. She knew these trees; their
roots jutted high above the ground in part, forming enclo-
sures in which a couple could sit or lie at ease. Josephine
knew this tree as well as she knew her own house. Her voice
came to Psyche: 'Let's sit here, darling, and make love to
one another. We are far from everyone.'

Psyche too halted abruptly. Then, gingerly, she worked
her way to the opposite side of the path and crept to the rear
of the spot where Charles Huntingdon and Josephine
reclined. She listened; see she could not; but presently she
guessed that Josephine had thrown herself in the young
man's arms, and that she was whispering, whispering in his
ear. A wave of jealousy and hate flooded the heart of the
listener; she was a savage stark and furious at that moment,
an African woman in a frenzy of hate. But she could do
nothing, did not dare let her presence be suspected; she still
had sufficient self-control to check her impulse to fling herself upon Josephine. Did she dare do so, she knew that the
white girl would have had her flogged that very night,
flogged without mercy, even should the squire plead for
her. So she remained all ears, and her limbs grew stiff, for
she hardly dared to move. Thus an hour passed, and at last
the two rose and made their way to the house, and to the
guests who still caroused in the dining-room.

She took the way back to Hope Vale. She knew that the
white girl, Josephine Brookfield, had become the 'wife' of
Charles Huntingdon. She felt that it would not be long now
before, at Josephine's demand, she would be shifted to the
slave village and perhaps made to work as a field hand on
the plantation where she had queened it for these long
months.

Chapter 7

AT THE GREAT HOUSE

ON TUESDAY Josephine came again to spend a few days with Mrs. Buxton. This was part of her plan. She brought with her the man Mashimba as a servant; Plimsole could spare him for a time. She rode into Hope Vale with a triumphant air; she considered herself as being, in a manner of speaking, almost mistress of that establishment, for had its master not become her lover?

'He loves me, Ida,' she said to Mrs. Buxton, for the first time addressing that lady by her Christian name; 'he is mine for good, and now he must get rid of that nagar slave he has, and you must look after the Great House when I am not here.'

Josephine knew what she had next to do. Between twelve and one o'clock that day she betook herself to the Great House, going boldly up to the front door and walking into the house when the door was opened. Charles was taking lunch at the time. He had not expected her; this manœuvre on her part took him by surprise.

Psyche was waiting on him, as usual. She stared at the visitor. Josephine was possessive in manner and entirely self-confident. 'I have come to stay awhile with Mrs. Buxton,' she announced, 'and I dropped in to see you. You don't mind, Squire, do you?' This was unusual, for class distinctions were strictly observed even if the opposite sexes were privately on terms of the utmost intimacy. But Huntingdon could only reply: 'Of course not: will you have some lunch?' And Josephine readily consented.

She had not so much as glanced at Psyche as she came into the room. Now she sat at the table while the black girl waited on her, affecting not to observe the embarrassment of Mr. Huntingdon. She ordered what she wanted, taking care to help herself to none of the things which Psyche first handed to her. She wished to begin her reign by giving commands to a menial, a menial who was also a slave. Once she spoke sharply, as though Psyche had made an avoidable mistake. Then, the meal over, she asked Huntingdon could she stay in the house with him for a couple of hours. It was all openly, brazenly done. He hesitated one moment, then said that he would be pleased if she remained. She looked at Psyche pointedly. 'We shall no longer need you, Psyche,' he said.

The slave girl bowed silently and left the room, then Josephine rose and went to the squire's chair. He had pushed it back from the table; she squeezed herself into his lap and put her arm around his neck. She bent him down and kissed him. 'I missed you,' she murmured, 'so I come here to see you. Are you glad to see me, Mr. Charles?'

He did not quite like her attitude of possession: indeed, he had been regretting the incident of Saturday night, feeling that he was slipping, feeling that he must get a hold upon himself before he reached the bottom of the slope— drinking and promiscuity and a brutal disregard for the feelings of others. But now he realised that Josephine had no intention that he should pause on his downward slide; her presence today was proof of that. She kissed him again and again as though she loved him passionately, as though there were no one within a mile of them, though only a few yards away were Psyche and the other servants. The warmth of her body, the passion of her caresses, sent a fever through him: he found himself responding to her fervour; soon he felt as indifferent as she did as to who might be within call, careless of the fact that there were men and women about who, if they could not see, nevertheless knew that behind the closed door of the dining-room were a young man and young woman, meeting privately, probably making love: both of them white, both of them set high above the bondspeople of the estate. For the slaves knew by this where he had gone last Saturday night: Psyche's eyes were not the only ones which had seen Josephine and Charles Huntingdon steal away into the cane farm at midnight.

'Don't go out now,' she whispered; 'stay with me; stay with me forever.'

'But you can't live in this house, Jose,' he pointed out weakly. 'Your father could not allow that; it is one of the things that few white women do in this country, I believe.'

'I love you, and I don't care for anything else,' she answered. 'But I could live in Montego Bay if you like, and you could come there and see me—often. And I could come here and stay with Mrs. Buxton every now and then, and come over in the evening to see you. Nobody could say anything to that: and if they want to do so, let them. I am here today, tomorrow, and Thursday, and I am going to come here night after night unless you don't want me to. But perhaps you don't want me to?' she enquired. 'They say, you know, that Psyche is your housekeeper.'

How distasteful all this was, he thought. He ignored her last remark.

'You know I want you to come,' he said, and felt that he had taken an irrevocable plunge downwards. 'That's what I want you to say,' she cried triumphantly.

She had left Mashimba to shift for himself outside. The Mandingo caught sight of Psyche brooding by an open window at the back and attracted her attention. She beckoned to him and he went up to her: he sensed that something was afoot to make her unhappy.

He spoke some English now; it was in that tongue that he addressed her.

'Miss Josephine is wit' de master, Miss Psyche; dis is de firs' time she come at Hope Vale two weeks runnin'.'

'She come for him, Mashimba, as you know. She wants to take him an' to turn me out.'

'Didn't I tell y'u so?'

'Yes.'

'What y'u goin' to do?'

'What can I do?'

He dropped into his native dialect: 'You were a priestess in our own country,' he said, 'and you could bring the rain and save us from starvation. You were powerful. Is the white girl more powerful than you?'

She thought. 'I don't know,' she said at length, dejectedly.

'I believe you had a strong magic, and you spoke the other day when you came to Plimsole as if you had. Now——'

'The power of white people is stronger than ours, Mashimba; I see that now. But you are right; I have a strong magic and she hasn't got the squire yet. If only I had a child!'

'A child! But our people don't sacrifice children, Psyche; we never do that; it is accursed.'

'I mean a child for him,' she replied patiently. 'Perhaps it would be different then, I don't know. But it is too late now to think about that. Hurry away now, Mashimba, lest she see me talking to you. Come tonight to that door'—she pointed to the attached outbuilding which she had kept as hers.

Mashimba went away, and she remained at the window thinking. She had been so confident of her hold over the squire even after she had first visited Plimsole; she was shaken to the foundations of her being in that conviction now. Yet she would have to fight. She felt it, knew it; the alternative for her was too terrible. She would have to fight; but how?

She heard Josephine's voice calling her imperatively; only then did she realise that she had stood at that window for nearly three hours, neglecting her chores, dwelling over and over again on the single problem that occupied her mind.

She hastened to obey the call.

'You,' said Josephine peremptorily, 'I want you to see that the squire's room is nicely cleaned at once; it smells funny; it's disgusting! it is filthy! And put clean sheets on the bed, you hear? I suppose you are head servant in this place?'

'Yes,' said Psyche.

'Yes, missis,' rapped out Josephine; 'do you forget you'self? Answering me "yes" like that! What a piece of forwardness! And you wearing shoes too: that's a joke! Now, make no mistake about the room. I . . . I shall be here tonight, you understand?'

'You mean to say . . .'

'Never mind what I mean to say: what I mean to say have nothing to do with a slave gal! But if you want to know, I can tell you I am going to be here tonight and tomorrow night, and Thursday night also, and I am going to sleep in the squire's room with the squire, and you will bring in coffee at six o'clock, for I shall be leaving about then. And the squire won't have no black slut sleeping with him again: the proper place for people like you is the cane field. That's what I mean to say. And I shall be here for supper tonight, an' if you open you' mouth to say one word that I say to you now, I will never rest till I have you damn' well flogged. That's what I mean to say. Now clear out.'

Silently Psyche turned to obey, knowing that the other's eyes dwelt on her scornfully and with intense dislike. And this was but the beginning. There was probably worse to come.

Chapter 8

PSYCHE DECIDES

PSYCHE did not wait at table that evening; her master told her it was not necessary: he wished to spare her feelings. Two men servants did so; the result was some awkwardness and blundering which Mr Huntingdon noticed, if Miss Brookfield did not.

Psyche hovered about the kitchen while dinner was being prepared and served, and already she observed the altered demeanour of the other domestic slaves. These no longer treated her with deference but merely as one of themselves; and those who felt they had a grievance because of her sneered at her openly and even presumed to speak sharply to her. She flared up at them, and that awed them into silence. After all, it came to their minds, they did not know yet how far she had fallen from the master's grace.

She remembered that Miss Brookfield (whom her fellow-slaves already spoke of as 'the young missis' in servile tones) had ordered her to serve coffee at six the following morning. By then Mr. Huntingdon would have left the house, since very early hours for both white men and black was the rule on all estates. But Psyche was not disposed to listen abjectly to any more of Josephine's rudeness. She would not take in that young lady's coffee. She would prefer to be flogged—though she felt certain that Mr. Huntingdon would never consent to her undergoing such a punishment.

She was crouching at the threshold of the little outhouse that night, dinner being long over and darkness supervening, when Mashimba quietly stole up to her as directed. No one saw him. He squatted on the ground at Psyche's feet. She said to him casually:

'You wait on the young mistress at her place sometimes, don't you, Mashimba?'

'Yes,' he answered, speaking as she did in his African tongue, 'though shortly I shall have to go to cut canes in the fields.'

'Come here tomorrow morning early, before six o'clock, and take in her coffee then; she would prefer someone she knows.'

'But I am a stranger here,' he objected; 'unless she says she wants me.'

'No; she wants me; but I can't do it, Mashimba; I am not going to do it. She would abuse me, perhaps strike me, and I could do nothing. She has taken away my master already, now she wants to wipe her feet on my face. I can't stand that. I would strike her in return, perhaps kill her. And then——'

'Very well,' he interrupted quickly, 'I will come; but suppose she says she don't want me to wait upon her?'

'Then one of the other slaves here will have to do it. I won't. I don't care what they do to me—I won't.'

'And afterwards?' he asked. He was conscious of a feeling of disappointment in Psyche. He thought that, considering what she was in her own land, and her confident boasts when he had first met her at Plimsole, she would have been able to demonstrate her 'power', shown that she was not helpless even before a white woman. But she was now like all the rest of them, submissive to her fate, even if she was putting up some sort of fight against becoming the body-servant of his mistress.

'There is no afterwards,' she answered dully, 'unless the master gets tired of her. Do you think he will, Mashimba?'

'She is white and you are black,' he replied boldly. 'You were only for a time, and so long as he didn't know her. It is bad for you now, but in a little while it will be worse. You are going to the cane fields, daughter, as I am.'

She noticed he did not say 'Priestess', addressed her by

no title of honour. Yet, in this land, where the slaves craved to maintain some sort of pretence that they were great people in Africa, they were usually scrupulous in respecting the dignity of those who were not common folk in their own countries. On the other hand the term 'daughter' implied affection in this man. She felt that he loved her as though she were his own flesh and blood.

'Better go now,' she suggested; 'it won't help us if people should see us together. She would prevent you even speaking to me if she saw you.'

He went at that word, truly sorry for her, even grieving, but feeling her case to be hopeless.

The following morning, Josephine being dressed and ready to leave the Great House by six o'clock, he took her morning coffee into her. She was in the dining-room; Mr. Huntingdon had left half an hour before. Neither Josephine nor Mashimba knew that Psyche had waited on him. Nor had Psyche said anything to him about what had happened. She noticed, though, that the squire avoided her eyes. Had she been a keener reader of faces she would also have observed that on his countenance were depicted uneasiness, remorse and shame.

For Josephine had told him she had ordered Psyche to bring in her coffee in the morning, and Josephine had even suggested that the girl should now be sent to labour in the fields. 'I don't want her to be in the house with you, Mr. Charles,' Josephine had said emphatically, 'and you won't want her to be here if you love me. Turn her away; she is robbing you, I have no doubt.'

'No, Jose, she's not robbing me,' he had replied, 'and she has been here almost ever since she came to Hope Vale.'

'But now it is different, darling,' she had whispered; 'you didn't know me then. And she is a nigger an' a savage: you can't love her. And I love you. You must send her away, you hear?'

Weakly he had promised that he would, but decided that it would not be to the cane fields. Perhaps Mrs. Buxton would take her on in her house; if he ordered Buxton to see that that was done, there would be no further talk about the matter. He mentioned this decision to Josephine, fearing that she would argue and protest against it. To his surprise and pleasure she readily agreed.

Josephine fascinated him, already had begun to dominate him. And Psyche was only a slave. But he remembered that he had cared for her, and he could not rid himself of the feeling that, no matter what other masters in Jamaica might do, he was a gentleman by birth and breeding and had a standard of honour rather different from that which prevailed amongst those around him.

'I suppose that nigger slut ordered you to bring in me coffee,' said Jose to Mashimba as he entered the dining-room that morning, and he meekly answered: 'Yes, missis.'

'Well, you can tell her from me that after this week she is going to Mrs. Buxton's house and will catch hell there, as she know. It will even be worse than going to the cane field, where some "bookkeeper" might pick her for his woman. She will have to scrub floor and wash clothes and work from morning to night until her face look like old plantain skin. Tell her I say so. She is you' relative, no?'

'No, missis, she not related to me,' said Mashimba.

'So much the better for you; yet when she say so at Plimsole, you didn't deny it. Why you people love to lie an' t'ief so, eh?'

She didn't pause for an answer, but went on chattering, while she poured her coffee into the saucer, blew on the liquid loudly with her breath, and swallowed it. Then she hurried off while still the January morning was dark. Mrs. Buxton, she guessed, would be delighted to learn that in a few days at most Psyche would be coming to her as a slave domestic. Mrs. Buxton would easily be able to find enough faults in Psyche that would justify physical punishment at fairly frequent intervals. It was just such an opportunity as would give pleasure to Mrs. Buxton's heart.

That night Mashimba told Psyche what Josephine had said to him. Psyche, who had continued to wait on table when Mr. Huntingdon was in the house, had noticed the malignant glances shot at her that evening by Josephine, the air of triumph which that young lady wore. Now she knew the reason. She knew also that work in the cane fields, though it would be to her a terrible humiliation, would be much preferable to being under the direct commands of Mrs. Buxton. That would be simply unbearable now. Her fate would be worse than any she had formerly contemplated.

She made up her mind to speak to the squire about it. But would he change his decree, with the white mistress urging him to stand firm and perhaps insisting that there was no pleasing this spoilt slave girl? That was doubtful. The upshot of her pleading might only be the disgusting of the man who had liked her once. Her dilemma was terrible. She buried her face in her hands, but she did not weep. She was thinking.

Suddenly she lifted her head.

'You will come to me tomorrow night as usual, Mashimba?' she asked the man. 'You go back to Plimsole on Friday morning, you know.'

'I will come to say goodbye,' he promised, and she nodded satisfaction. Then she sent him away.

The cook-house or kitchen of Hope Vale was usually deserted after two o'clock in the afternoon, though on the huge brick fireplace embers always glowed. About two o'clock the next day Psyche slipped into the little room she now inhabited, carefully closed every aperture opening upon the yard, raised quietly a loosened board which formed part of the flooring of the room, and drew from a hole dug in the earth, and lightly covered with dirt, a tiny bag of cloth. From this bag she extracted two beans: there were ten in all, and she had brought them with her from Africa and hidden them ever since. She was acquainted with their properties; she knew that they were potent even after many years; that some of them were kept for much longer that she had lived and yet were in effect as though they had been gathered the day before. Toast them, grind them to powder, and mix them into paste, smear the paste on the spears of hunters that went out to slay big game, and once the poison had entered the flesh there was no hope for the largest and strongest of animals. For the poison killed surely if slowly, and there was no antidote for it. To be cut or stabbed, or even bruised with something on which it had been rubbed, meant certain death.

And she it was who, as priestess of her village, had to make this poison—her people called it magic. She had been taught to do it. And knowing the effect of the poison upon beasts and men, she had felt herself a woman of power.

But administered in drink? Would it be efficacious then? She had heard of those who had slain men in that fashion, though she herself had never done so. She would know in a little while if that report were true.

She sauntered into the kitchen, hastily toasted the couple of beans over the embers in an iron spoon, went back to her room and powdered them by rubbing another iron spoon against them. She was skilled in this sort of thing, and the work was easy. She carefully shook the powder into an envelope she had taken from Mr. Huntingdon's study, placed it in her bosom, and hid the spoons under the floor of her apartment, intending to throw them in the river when she had the chance. Then she waited patiently until night and Mashimba should come.

When he made his appearance she went to the point at once.

'Mashimba,' she said, 'I was powerful in our own country: you remember?'

'Yes, my daughter, but powerless here.'

'That is not so, Mashimba; I but pretended to have no magic because I wanted to see if you still believed in me. Perhaps you don't; but now you will see shortly whether I am lying to you or not. You wait on the young mistress sometimes at Plimsole, as you do here, don't you?'

'Yes; sometimes.'

'Very well. Either Saturday morning, or whenever you can, soon after that, take her in her morning coffee. But before you do so, put this powder in it; it has no taste. You promise?'

'What is it, Priestess?' he asked, struck by the urgency of her manner, by her confident claim to power at a moment when he had expected despondency and a submissive spirit.

'It is some of my magic. If she takes it she will be separated from my master forever; he will want to have nothing to do with her again.'

'But if she wants to have something to do with him?'

'She will not: that is the magic. And, Mashimba?'

'Yes, Priestess?'

'No one must see you put the powder in the young mistress's coffee—not a soul. And when no one is looking, burn the envelope in which it is. And, whatever happens, say no word to anyone; not a word, mind. If you do you will have serious trouble, and I will never forgive you.'

'Is it—is it something to kill?' he whispered.

'And if it were,' she said, 'you would not do what I ask?' There was a threat in her voice.

'I would do it,' he answered, 'for I hate that woman also. And you—are you not of my own country and people?'

'Good.'

'But I could put the magic in her coffee tomorrow before

we leave here,' he suggested. 'I may have a better chance.'

'No,' she hissed. 'not here; anywhere but here. Plimsole is best.'

'It will be as you say,' he agreed.

'Go now, and the gods of our country prosper you.'

Chapter 9

FAILURE OR SUCCESS?

THAT Saturday was the worst that Psyche had ever spent in Jamaica. She had created jealousy, she had stirred up envy, she had even engendered hate in the hearts of some of her fellow-slaves; her downfall, therefore, now that it was plain, created far more joy than pity; even to those who felt no active enmity towards her it seemed only natural that she should give place to a missis who was almost as young as she was, and pretty, and, above all, white.

Some knew that Josephine was hard, was perhaps inclined to be cruel. But she was of the master's race and therefore privileged. Psyche had no rights and was clearly only a usurper; and Psyche also was inclined to be hard. Her dominance when in power had been secretly resented; her fall was therefore matter for satisfaction. Already one of the women on the estate who had heard of the coming of Miss Brookfield had composed a song that would soon be chanted by everyone when at work or play, a song of two lines merely, of which the words were:

> Guinea bud fly high,
> But Backra lady cut him wing, Oh!

She had begun to sing it already, laughing as she did so. Everybody who heard the song knew its implications. It was a taunt, an expression of scorn, and the slaves well knew that scorn and taunting were to one of their own people the bitterest insult that could be offered.

Would Mashimba succeed? That was the question in Psyche's mind all day long. He might be discovered, and that would mean his death, and hers too if he told how she had set him on. Or the poison might not work: it had not been rubbed upon a cutting instrument to enter directly into the blood stream, and that was the only way it had ever been potent, so far as she was certain, in distant Africa. Besides, here in Jamaica there were magicians who were called doctors, and they cured illnesses that puzzled Africans, and professed to know the causes of those illnesses. If they should discover what had killed Josephine it was hanging for her as well as for Mashimba. She shuddered at this thought. Yet she knew she would do again now what she had planned to do on Thursday. All that was hard and strong and determined in her nature came to the surface now that she was putting up the supreme fight of all her life.

Had Mashimba succeeded even in putting the powder into Miss Brookfield's drink? Again and again she asked herself that question.

As a matter of fact he had.

He made it his business to be early in the kitchen or cook-house of Mr. Brookfield's residence on the Saturday morning; he pretended to be making himself useful chopping wood, attending to the fire, and so forth; and as he had done this before his actions were not suspicious. Knowing too that he sometimes took in Miss Brookfield's early morning coffee, the cook had handed to him the steaming cup of it when it was ready and he had started off at once to take it in to her. In early January it is still dark at six in the morning in Jamaica; the kitchen too was situated at a little distance from the house, as was the custom on the estates. On his way with Josephine's morning beverage, therefore, he glanced about him; and as there seemed no one within eyeshot it was easy for him to take out of his trousers pocket the envelope which Psyche had given him, shake its contents quickly into the cup, slip the envelope back into his pocket, and, when he had set down the tray with the coffee on the dining-table, hastily stir the liquid until no trace of powder remained on its surface, and then wipe all signs of the liquid from the spoon. Jose ordinarily drank her early coffee in the dining-room; at seven o'clock she had some more coffee and a regular breakfast, and at eleven she ate a 'second breakfast', which was really the meal of the day for most free women in Jamaica. Mashimba never entered her bedroom when he brought in her coffee. Jose took no meals in bed.

She came out when he summoned her by a knock at her door; she poured milk into the coffee, added a little dark brown sugar, then emptied the fragrant mixture into a saucer and began to cool it with her breath. This was her custom; she also often, when alone, or with intimate friends, ate even meat with her fingers and would squat down on the floor to eat out of a pot. This was a habit of childhood to which she would now and then revert. Table manners were mostly company manners for people of her class, and crude.

Mashimba lingered in the dining-room, looking at her anxiously. Would she suddenly fall dead? It was only now that this question forcibly occurred to him; hitherto he had been thinking only of putting the 'magic' in her cup; he had given no thought as to what might be its immediate consequences. He had dwelt upon his first step only; now that that had been taken he felt considerable alarm. If he were suspected. . . but he had faith in Psyche. She had been a priestess, therefore she was still one in his eyes. She could protect him from harm.

Josephine finished her coffee, then suddenly asked Mashimba how he would like it if Mr. Huntingdon bought him from the attorney of Plimsole. She saw that the question surprised him.

'I will be often at Hope Vale now,' she said complacently, 'and I would like one or two of the people I know here to be there too. Now that I know you are not related to that slut, Psyche, I may get Mr. Huntingdon to buy you. You would like that, eh?'

Naturally, he answered yes. Whether he would like this transference or not, it would take place if the price offered for him were sufficiently tempting. He was only being asked his opinion because his mistress was in a gracious mood this morning.

'You say you not related to that nagar gal at Hope Vale?'

'No, missis.'

'Then how y'u come to know her?'

'We come on de same ship, missis.'

'I see. Well, I want you to belong to Hope Vale. Psyche will be a slave in Mrs. Buxton house, an' instead of riding horse an' wearing stocking she will have to scrub floor with coconut brush, and wear osnaburg. That's all she fit for. And I want some of the people who come to Jamaica with her to see it; you in particular, as she seem to teck you for a friend. But, you hear, you mustn't even speak to her at Hope Vale. You hear?'

'Yes, missis.'

'An' you must watch her, and if she say anything or do anything to get near to the massa, you must let me know as soon as you can. You hear?'

'Yes, missis.'

'And I will treat you well, for you getting old. Though you people are so damn ungrateful that sometimes it seem useless to do anything for you.'

As she was inclined to be familiar, he ventured to ask her a question. 'You gwine to live with the massa at Hope Vale, missis?'

'Of course not, you big fool,' she laughed. 'I am a white lady, an' I couldn't live out-an'-out with a gentleman. But I will come often an' often to Hope Vale to see me friend, Mrs. Buxton, an' I will be the real missis of the place. You understand now?'

He nodded comprehension. Indeed, he knew that this was how it was already. He was greatly relieved too that she had not fallen dead before him, and in fact appeared to be no wise the worse for Psyche's 'magic'. The access of fear that had swept upon him, the terrible reaction, now ebbed, but he felt strangely weak. He said to himself that the white man's magic was more powerful than that of the black man.

Josphine went about in high good humour that forenoon; she was dwelling on her golden prospects. She ate her 'second breakfast' with a hearty appetite as usual, not giving a thought to the fact that, if she continued to feed herself as she was doing, she would be fat at thirty and so lose the splendid figure of which she was now inordinately proud. At one o'clock she went for her usual siesta. She fell asleep thinking of Charles Huntingdon. He was hers now, and she would bend his mind to her purposes.

When she awoke at three she was conscious of a numbness in her feet. It was slight, but unaccustomed. She paid no attention to it; but an hour later, when dawdling over the meal called dinner, she noticed that the numbness had crept up to her legs; she mentioned the fact to her father.

'You must have caught a cold in your legs,' he diagnosed. 'You are very careless.'

She agreed good-humouredly and took no further notice of her trifling complaint.

At ten o'clock that night, after they had gone to bed, her father heard her calling to him loudly.

'I am frightened,' she gasped, when he rushed into her room. 'I am numb up to here'—she pointed to her stomach —'and I can't move my legs and my arms are heavy. I am sick. For God's sake, send for a doctor.'

Her face was distorted by fear: he dared not argue with her though he thought she was exaggerating. But this was Saturday night, and to get a doctor from Montego Bay now might be no easy undertaking. However, he ran out and ordered Mashimba, the first slave he encountered, to hasten to the Bay at once and bring a doctor. 'Take a horse,' commanded Mr. Brookfield, 'and ride like hell.'

He summoned two or three female slaves: these applied

hot towels to Josephine's body and limbs; one of them threw herbs—'wild bush' as she called them—into a cauldron, proposing to boil them and to bathe Jose with the concoction. No one knew what had happened, but the suddenness of the attack seemed to them mysterious; they whispered among themselves; the word 'obeah' was muttered again and again. 'Are you in any pain?' asked Mr. Brookfield of his daughter, as she lay on the bed unable to move.

'No,' she replied faintly; 'not at all. But I can't move. I can't move.'

Meantime Mashimba rode swiftly to Montego Bay, and his brain hummed with but one thought. The magic was taking effect; the magic was working. But it did not seem to mean death; perhaps, when the young missis' sickness was over, she would turn with distaste from Massa Huntingdon, and he from her: perhaps Psyche had given the massa a similar drink. At any rate no one suspected him, Mashimba, of having had anything to do with the matter. Otherwise Mr. Brookfield would not have sent him to fetch the doctor.

Mashimba was lucky; the doctor was found at home. He grumblingly consented to go to Plimsole, although he was not the usual medico—who was merely a dispenser—of that estate. He arrived at about midnight; he was told that Josephine's numbness had crept steadily upwards, and must have reached her heart. She had died an hour ago.

It was midday Sunday before the news reached Hope Vale, and this was only because Mrs. Buxton had been a friend of Josephine's. Otherwise a week might have passed and no one on Hope Vale might have heard of the event. Mashimba, however, was sent with the tidings to Mrs. Buxton; it seemed to that lady as if a thunderbolt had struck her. It was incredible. On Friday morning Josephine was bidding her goodbye, strong, healthy, in the flush of her youth and beauty, the accepted mistress of the squire, the prospective wielder of power on Hope Vale estate. Now she was lying cold and dead, and not even the doctor knew what it was that had killed her.

Mrs. Buxton would go to the funeral: her husband's trap would take her over in time. Jose was to be buried that afternoon: her body could not longer be kept uninterred in such a climate.

Mrs. Buxton went herself to inform the squire of the tragedy that had occurred; with real tears in her eyes she told him of the sudden ending of her young friend's life. 'An' no one know what cause it, Squire,' she said. 'She just dead so.'

Charles Huntingdon was startled, shocked. His face whitened; for a moment he could articulate no word. Yet he was conscious, shamefacedly, of a curious feeling of relief. It was as though shackles, which had been fastened upon him, were unexpectedly struck off. 'Thank you for coming to tell me this awful news,' he said courteously at length, as soon as he mustered his voice; 'it is dreadful. Poor girl! Of course, I will go to the funeral.' Then with bowed shoulders, he went into his room.

What had caused Josephine's death, he wondered. And would there be an inquest? Death came only too quickly in this country; it followed one like a perpetual shadow; it was the constant spectre at the feast of life. But Josephine? Surely there was something strange in her swift ending.

She had become his mistress, through his own weakness, he felt. Why had he grown so weak? But for him, would this tragedy have occurred?

Had Psyche? . . . But how? No; that thought must be dismissed. In this thing, surely, she could have had no hand. But how, how, how?

Mrs. Buxton too asked herself what had killed her friend; again and again the question rang in her mind. It wasn't yellow fever. It couldn't be arsenic either, for Mashimba had said positively that there was no pain and no vomiting. Then what?

Good God, what could it be? For the sudden death of this handsome girl did not seem natural, there was something devilish about it. She had been murdered. By whom and by what means?'

The domestics of the Hope Vale Great House heard the news; and they too wondered. On Friday the missis had been there; on Saturday night she was dead. She had displaced Psyche. Then . . . Then?

Then they saw Psyche going about her work as usual, work which had changed somewhat during the past two weeks, but which was not markedly menial. And they noted her air. It was not one of relief merely; that would be natural. For now she might well hope to be restored to the white massa's favour. It was not an air even of thankful satisfaction: no one could blame her for that. But her gait was swaggering, arrogant, triumphant; her eyes blazed with conscious fire of power, she spoke as though she expected to be obeyed, she gave orders; she was not the young woman of yesterday. The others saw, were frightened, and whispered 'obeah'. They had all heard that, in her own part of Africa, Psyche had been a priestess.

There was no reason why Psyche should go that afternoon in the direction of Mrs. Buxton's house. Yet she did so, just when Mrs. Buxton was setting forth for Josephine's funeral. Incongruously enough, she had dressed in one of the low-cut frocks that had been bought a year ago, and she wore the shoes she had discarded during the last two weeks. She saw Mrs. Buxton as that lady was about to leave for Plimsole, and she insolently gazed full into her eyes, making no sort of curtsy, not moving her lips in humble salutation, but holding high her head. Mrs Buxton glared at her, then heard the low scornful laugh that came from the slave girl's lips. 'It's that black wretch that kill Josephine!' gasped Mrs. Buxton; 'but how?' and into her mind, also, crept the word 'obeah'. For in those days white as well as black believed that there might be something in the savage's dark and mysterious cults.

It came to Mrs. Buxton at this moment, too, that if this girl could kill Josephine Brookfield so ruthlessly, so mysteriously, and at such a distance, there were others that she could kill also.

And Mrs. Buxton was afraid.

Chapter 10

AT LAST

'SQUIRE, I have something to tell you.'

Psyche knelt beside the squire, who, in the intense heat of the summer afternoon, was reclining on the sheltered verandah of the Great House in a huge leathern armchair, a small table at his side whereon was a tall tumbler filled with rum punch. He had discarded his jacket; his soft shirt was open at the neck; he looked a little fatter than he had done some months before but had not lost that look of distinction which marked him out from among most of the other leading planters of his parish, or, indeed, of the island.

'Well, say it, Psyche: is it anything important?'

'Squire, you wouldn't want any child of yours to be a slave, would you?'

'Good Lord, no, Psyche! But why do you ask that? You have no children.'

'No and yes.'

'No and yes? That sounds like nonsense; no, but——' he sat erect suddenly. 'Just what do you mean?' he asked in a strange tone of voice.

'I am going to have a child, Squire. I know it positively now. I thought so more than a month ago; now I know it. At last.'

'Great heavens!'

'You're vexed?'

'How could I be vexed at something neither you nor I could prevent? I have foreseen this possibility for long. But it creates certain problems, Psyche. You see that?'

'Problems?' It was clear that she did not understand the implications of the word, did not realise what he could possibly mean. Then she asked: 'If you are not vexed, are you pleased?'

At the moment he could not answer her truthfully. He turned the question over in his mind. Was he pleased? He felt no pleasure at her announcement, though he knew he had been expecting it for months and months, that it was something any man would have expected, and that then the matter had simply faded from his mind. He understood, too, why she had asked whether he would like any child of his to be a slave. A great many white men in the country had to face that question at one time or the other. They answered it usually by making their children free.

'No, Psyche,' he answered after a few moments of silence, 'your child—and mine—will not be a slave.'

'I knew that,' she replied in a tone of satisfaction. 'Then when will you make me free?'

'You? Well, I thought you were happy and satisfied; that you wished to be always with me.'

'Yes; always. But if you died, Squire, before I did?'

'That has never occurred to me, I confess; but you are right. Once you are free you are free forever. So that if I died and you had children by some other man they also would be free. Is that what you are thinking about?'

'You know it is not, Squire. If you died I would have no more children; I wouldn't have any other man. You know that. But my children—and yours—must be born *free*, and you can see that they are. Am I right?'

'I will go down to Montego Bay tomorrow and arrange for the drawing up of your manumission papers, Psyche: that won't take long. And then you can do as you please, no one preventing you. It is curious that I never thought of making you free before; you see, it seemed to me that here you were really your own mistress and were quite contented. But I have been selfish, or, at least unthinking. As a matter of fact,' he added bitterly, 'I would like to set free every slave on this property. I hate slavery.'

'But you must have people to make sugar, Squire, and these slaves don't know any better. What more do they want? But I am to be free, and our children will be free!' She sprang upright. 'And I too will have slaves, and property in time, and'—she hesitated a little, but the words had to come—'and nobody will try to again take you from me, Squire, for they can't succeed.'

This oblique reference to Josephine Brookfield was almost the first she had made to that unfortunate girl since the tragedy on Plimsole some six months before. He understood her, but offered no comment, and she fell gently back to the floor, sitting, not kneeling now, wondering whether she had said too much.

Mechanically his hand wandered to her shoulder and rested there. A child? He the son of aristocrats, he who might some day return to his native land? He would have to leave behind his Jamaica children, perhaps would never see them again, as happened to so many other men in the land. But would he want to leave them? Would he be strong enough, or sufficiently indifferent, to do that?

She too was thinking. She remembered that Sunday when news of Josephine's sudden death had been brought to Hope Vale. She had seen something in Mrs. Buxton's manner that warned her of Mrs. Buxton's suspicions. But the doctor that had gone to Plimsole too late—not that, in any case, he could have done anything for Josephine—had made little fuss about the death: he had talked something about heart disease, and no one was sufficiently knowledgeable or influential to say that his opinion was nonsensical. There was no inquest; there seemed no reason why there should be any; and, had there been, it would have resulted in nothing.

As for Psyche, she felt not a twinge of remorse for what she had done. It seemed to her right and proper that she should have removed a dangerous rival by the only means in her power: she was pleased and proud that her plan had gone so well. And because she was quick-witted, she realised within a week of the occurrence that the people on Hope Vale believed that, in some sort of way, it was she who had struck down Josephine Brookfield and consequently stood in great awe of her. She saw this in the frightened attitude of Mrs. Buxton as well as in the deferential, in fact cringing, behaviour of the slaves. They were talking about her, she knew; but she deemed this more of an advantage than otherwise. They might suspect anything, but they knew nothing; the one person on Hope Vale that she did not want to get suspicious was the master, and soon she was satisfied that he did not suspect her.

She wore shoes continually now, she dressed every day in European costume, she tried more and more to talk as her master did, despising the broken English, the peculiar dialect, of the slave people. She was definitely 'Missis' to all the slaves. No one of them dared to speak to her by her christian name. No one desired to do so.

And now there was a child coming at long last. It must be born free, and to ensure that she herself must be made free.

In a few weeks it was done. She was a free woman, and under the law she too could now own slaves if she had the money to buy them. She could be a mistress in reality, and not merely by deputy. She knew that. And why not? she asked herself.

'Squire,' she said to Mr. Huntingdon one night, when she sat at his feet on a low stool after he had dined—for never, once, had she presumed even to speak to him as to an equal, easy-going and kind-natured though he was—'Squire, will you buy Mashimba for me?'

'Buy Mashimba: who is he?'

'They call him Homer at Plimsole, where he is a slave. He is from my village, and came over on the ship with me. He is an old man now, Squire, and he would be happier here. If you would give him to me . . .'

'As your own property, you mean?'

'Yes, I am a free woman now, but I haven't a thing: and I am going to have a child, so, you see, I want something. Don't you understand?'

'And is this man, Mashimba, all you want, Psyche?'

Her condition was quite apparent in these days, and he felt increasingly a responsibility that had caused him to do a good deal of thinking of late. As she was silent he resumed the conversation.

'If I give you Mashimba, that won't be very much in the circumstances, will it be?'

'But you will give me more when the baby—your baby— is born,' she answered. 'But I would like Mashimba, and he would like to come to me too.'

'I'll see if the people at Plimsole will sell him; they will hardly refuse if he is an old man, as you say. But we have to think of other things as well as Mashimba now. When your child is born I will buy for it a small property near here: the law, you know, does not allow me to leave any child in the position of yours more than twelve hundred pounds in money or property. I have an idea,' he laughed, 'that I told you that long ago when you first proposed to be one of my "wives". In fact,' he added almost gaily, 'when I come to think of it, it is you who seem to have done all our courting, Psyche.'

She nodded affirmatively. 'You wouldn't, so I had to do it. I am glad. Are you sorry, Squire?'

'No, not now.'

'I didn't understand you when you talked to me so long ago about children; but I understand you now. But don't you see, Squire, if you give every child I have a property or twelve hundred pounds'—the sum of money mentioned seemed an unimaginable fortune to her—'they will all be rich?'

'And suppose you don't have more than one child, Psyche?'

'I will have twenty.'

'Suppose, I say, you have only one.'

'But there is nothing, Squire, to prevent you giving me anything—money, I mean—you like. You are rich. Give me money now, and whenever you can afford it. I will keep it for my children. What can the law do about that?'

Nothing, he felt; and was also convinced of something else. He believed that any money he gave to her would be held in trust for her children, not wasted upon some other man. He thought the law limiting the amount which children of colour could receive from their fathers a foolish and iniquitous one; besides, the very men who made that law evaded it in just such ways as the one which Psyche suggested. The law was a sheer piece of hypocrisy and continually set at nought. He was angry as he thought of it. 'Very well,' he concluded; 'I think I shall do as you say.'

Chapter 11

DESTINY

SHE was free, she had property, she was twenty years of age, and had been in Jamaica for three years. Her child was healthy, bright, and now it could be seen that it was lighter in complexion than a pure mulatto would be; the semitic blood of Psyche's grandfather, which Psyche herself showed in her features and hair but not in her hue, was evidenced in her baby, who in later years would in Jamaica be considered a quadroon. It was one year old now, the mother and father saw in it future beauties that no one else perceived at present, and already Psyche was dreaming of a great career for her little one. She had hoped for a boy, but it was a girl that came. She had named it after herself. And because it was free she had added the father's name of Huntingdon. To this the squire had offered no objection. He himself indeed would have insisted on this had Psyche not suggested it.

Hope Vale had made money during these past few years; it was difficult for any sugar property decently administered not to make money out of sugar during the period of the Napoleonic Wars. With some of his savings Huntingdon had purchased in Psyche's name a large plot of good land adjoining his estate; later on he would leave to her and her girl as much as the law allowed and would give to the little child in the meantime what he could, even if that contravened the strict letter of the law. A house had been built on the land bought for Psyche, a small place in which she promptly installed a free Negro who understood much about cattle-raising. Her design was to breed cattle as beasts of burden for the surrounding estates; in her African village they had kept such stock, some of which frequently formed the purchase money for wives on the part of men who, by African standards, were wealthy. She herself knew something about cattle; Mashimba knew more. And now Mashimba was hers. He was her first slave. She had determined to acquire others, and when, because the slave trade had been prohibited at last, the price of human labourers rose considerably she still bought some by paying more than other buyers were inclined to do. And so the years slipped by, and Psyche became twenty-five years of age. Often she wondered at her material good fortune and happiness, and felt that it would never end.

The squire himself had grown a little stouter, and he was absorbed in his child. It was the only one; Psyche had begun to be frightened that she would have no more; sometimes she speculated as to the cause of this, for she believed, and would continue to her last day to believe, that many misfortunes experienced by human beings were caused by obeah or witchcraft, with malice or envy as its originating source. But these periods of fright or annoyance were short-lived; she reflected that she was still young; she knew of women who had borne children when older than herself; she fancied that white men often did not have children in quick succession. Happily, too, the squire didn't seem to mind that there was only one child. He was satisfied; but when little Psyche was six years of age the problem of her education confronted him.

He solved that temporarily by determining to teach her, himself, the rudiments of reading and writing. But later on, where was he to send her? There were no schools for her like within a radius of twenty miles; none into which she would be readily taken. And there were no suitable teachers, even if he decided to hire some dame to do nothing but undertake the instruction of his daughter. He thought vaguely about bringing out a teacher from England. That, at any rate, could be done.

Psyche had heard a strange kind of talk that was going about, had heard it occasionally, though no one seemed to believe it. The slave trade had ceased; it was now unlawful. And it was being said that slavery itself would cease, that a fight against it had long since begun in England, that in time everybody in Jamaica would be free. She thought such a suggestion monstrous: did she not herself own slaves? Would it be fair for anyone to rob her of her property? Did she not treat her people well; was not the master the kindest of men? And yet he hated slavery. Sometimes, when he was preoccupied, thinking of the future of their child, she imagined that it was these rumours of a possible coming emancipation that he was brooding upon. She felt that, though he would suffer loss, he would welcome it. She could not agree with this attitude; she failed to understand it.

December came, the estate was getting busy for the taking off of the cane crop and the manufacturing of sugar. Suddenly the squire seemed to abandon all interest in these important preparations. Psyche noticed this. She wondered what had happened.

'Something worrying you, Squire?'

It was after dinner, the darkness had fallen; on the veranda Mr. Huntingdon was seated in his favourite armchair; he sat here at nights when he was not reading: when he was, of course, he wanted to be quite alone.

Psyche sat on a sort of cushion at his feet; in one of the bedrooms the child lay asleep, watched over by a young female slave who now performed the functions of a nurse. In the sitting-room, which was never used, but in which the central chandelier was always lighted after dark, night insects hummed and whirled around the shaded candles; from the slave village came muted sounds that carried far; occasionally the sharp bark of a dog was heard. For an hour the squire had sat thinking, uttering not a word.

He did not answer her immediately even now; after

waiting awhile she repeated her question. 'Why do you ask that?' he said.

'Because you walk about as if something is on your mind; something serious. What is it, Squire?'

'My brother in England is dead, Psyche; I got a letter some days ago.'

'And you are sorry he is dead?'

'Yes; but that is not why I am worrying; after all, I haven't heard from my people at home these many years now. But, you see, he was my elder brother, and though he was married he had no children.'

'You can write and say you are sorry, Squire, that is all you can do.'

'No; I am afraid I shall have to go home, Psyche; I succeed my brother, you know. I wish I didn't.'

'What do you mean, Squire?'

'I shall have to go home,' he said again, patiently. 'They expect that, and there is no way out of it. It's my duty.'

'Duty? But why? What is that?'

'I am afraid you wouldn't understand, Psyche. But my mother is still alive, and I have other relatives; and there is the continuance of the family name to consider—but you won't understand all this. It would have been different if my brother had left a child, But now . . .'

'If you go, will you come back, Squire?' she asked urgently, a suggestion of fear in her voice.

'I'll try to,' he answered, but she noticed that there was no conviction in his tone.

'You will leave me here, and little Psyche?' she asked heavily.

'I shall have to leave you; there is no way out of that. But I have been thinking of the child. . . . What would you say if I took her with me, Psyche?'

'She is small; she couldn't go alone with a man, Squire. But if I go along with you——'

'That is impossible,' he interrupted firmly. 'I can take the slave that nurses her; of course, the moment she sets foot in England she will be free. But you are the mother, and the child is mine; what should I have to say about you, Psyche, and what should I do with you?'

'And when will my little girl come back?'

Silence fell in the darkness; an expression of misery crept over Huntingdon's countenance. 'She would go to school in England,' he replied at length; 'she would not return to Jamaica until she was grown up; and then—do you think she would like to come back, Psyche?'

'No. Not if you were not here. But if you take her I shall be left alone, all alone; for something tells me, Squire, that you will never come back.'

'Don't think such nonsense; why should you say that?' he answered weakly.

'You think it yourself; you know it. Look at the different Englishmen who have gone to England since I came here. Which of them has come back? And I haven't another child.'

'Then you will prevent little Psyche from going with me? Do you mean that?'

Another fall of silence ensued, in the midst of which the droning of the night insects could be distinctly heard. Then Psyche spoke.

'She will go to a good school and learn to be a lady, Squire?'

'Of course.'

'And then, perhaps, she wouldn't like to know her mother; and you wouldn't like that either. . . . Yet'—she hurried on to prevent an interruption—'yet all that would be good for her, and I could work here and save money for her . . . she would be rich some day, with what you and I could do for her. . . . Rich. But I will be alone.'

'Perhaps——'

'Don't say it, Squire; I know what you are going to say.

I could get married; but after you? Oh, no. I will remain alone. When are you going, Squire?'

'About four months time. There will be things to do here, and anyhow I could not take little Psyche to England in the dead of winter.'

In the darkness he heard a sob.

Mr. Buxton was both pleased and annoyed; Mrs. Buxton delighted yet scandalised. The squire was going away; he was now a lord; it was never likely that he would return to Jamaica. And instead of appointing some outsider to be the estate's 'attorney' he proposed that Mr. Buxton should act in that capacity while still remaining overseer of Hope Vale. This meant that he would now live in the Great House, would receive a handsome commission on the profits made, would be his own boss, and have under him a sub-overseer who must obey his every command. So far, excellent: but in this delicious ointment there was one ugly fly.

The fly got into the ointment after the following conversation between Psyche and the squire very shortly after he had told her of his brother's death and of his plans.

'Who will look after your property after you have gone, Squire?' asked Psyche.

'I am thinking that Mr. Buxton will do as well as anyone else; in fact better. He has been here any number of years; he understands the work; he is about the only person I think I can depend on.'

'Yes, so long as you are here; but leave him alone and you don't know what may happen. You may lose everything in time.'

'Like so many others, eh? But what am I to do? All these attorneys are alike.'

'Couldn't you join me with him, Squire, to look after your interests—and little Psyche's!'

'Such a thing has never been known in Jamaica, my good girl; I am afraid it is impossible.'

'Is there a law against a free black woman, with property of her own, becoming an attorney?' asked Psyche anxiously.

'No; now that you ask that, I don't think there is. But you forget, Psyche, that while you speak English, and speak it very well, you only read and write it indifferently—I mean,' he explained hastily, 'you can read and write, for I have taught you: you insisted on that, didn't you? But——'

'I don't think Mr. Buxton reads and writes any better than me, Squire; and there is Mr. Dodds, the lawyer in Montego Bay, who helps me with my cattle pen. He is very kind. He could help me with anything I have to do concerning this place. Why not try it, Squire? Ask Mr. Dodds. If he says I can protect you from being robbed, it will be all right. He knows your law and I can always go to him.'

'Very well, Psyche, I'll see.'

Huntingdon consulted Mr. Dodds after this; he was anxious to do what he possibly could for Psyche, whom he probably would never see again. Mr. Dodds agreed that she could be made a sort of joint-attorney for Hope Vale, although such a thing had never been known before. There was no law to prevent her from acting along with Mr. Buxton, and he, Mr. Dodds, would do his best for her.

Then, as the weeks drew on, as spring approached, Psyche's face became drawn, at times almost haggard. She was losing the squire; she knew it was for ever. He would probably marry in England, might have children, white children: what would happen then to her own little girl? She lay awake at night asking herself that question; it was ever in her mind. This Jamaica property could not be left to her; the law said so; it was worth far, far more than a mere twelve hundred pounds—Psyche understood that now: she had learnt much about money and riches in the last few years. But what truth was there in that talk of universal freedom, which she had heard with impatience formerly, but which she now caught at as though it were a shining hope? Surely this law that blocked little Psyche as an inheritor now would be altered then, if not indeed before; and all Hope Vale could then become the child's.

It was one week before the squire would leave Hope Vale. Psyche was sitting at her usual place on the veranda one night; he thought her brave exceedingly to keep back tears and reproaches as she did.

'I am sorry I have to go, Psyche,' he said, breaking the silence; it was all that he could say.

'You have done a lot for me, Squire; I can't be ungrateful,' she replied. 'You know,' she added, 'I think that you and I shall live to be old, very old.'

'But what has that to do with my going away, girl?'

'Plenty. I shall never see you again. I may never see my child again. But perhaps, long before we are dead, everybody here may have freedom, and the laws you always speak of, Squire, may be changed. Am I right?'

'I think so. The freedom of everyone in this country I would rejoice at; and with freedom, if not indeed before, there must come a changing of the laws. That indeed is certain.'

'Then, Squire, will you promise me one thing?'

'What is it? '

'Make a will leaving this property to our child.'

'It would not be valid now, Psyche, whether made here or in England. But I can tell you this. I will make a will such as you want every year, so that if the laws of inheritance in Jamaica are changed—as they will be some day—little Psyche shall have Hope Vale unless I die before the will is valid. I will do more for her, too, much more; you may depend upon me. But I can see that on her inheritance of this property you have set your heart.'

'Yes, Squire; and she will get it. I feel certain of that.'

'I will send you, regularly, successive copies of the will. But, you understand, the property may not be worth much if a general emancipation comes.'

'It will be worth a lot,' she answered; 'I will work for it, and Mr. Buxton will work for it also.'

'I hope so; you must try to get on with him; he has promised to get on with you.'

'We shall work well together, Squire,' she answered quietly. Then she muttered to herself: 'Mr. Buxton will remember Josephine Brookfield.'

Chapter 12

THE PROMISE

THE Great House was lighted up this early April morning as it never had been before in Charles Huntingdon's time. In the darkness before sunrise there was within it a sound of busy movement as men and women gathered and brought out to the waiting vehicle the things that the squire would take with him to Kingston. The journey to the city would occupy four arduous days; the heavier luggage had been sent to the city by sea two days ago. The slaves on the estate all knew that Massa Huntingdon was leaving Jamaica for ever—that was the tale which had got about, and it was true. So from all parts of the property they were coming to bid him farewell, though normally they would have been preparing to flock to their daily routine tasks.

He wished to see them all, to wave to them goodbye; he had had that wish conveyed to them. So they gathered outside the Great House and waited for him; and they muttered amongst themselves that never again would they have a 'massa' so considerate and kind.

A mist rose from the river that flowed through Hope Vale; there was a chill in the morning air that would disappear when the sun shot up in a burst of golden glory, lighting plain and hillside, slave's hut and white man's house, heralding a new day's toil, ushering what would be for the people on the estate a new era, for another white man would rule there now and they wondered what sort of a master he would make with the owner far away in England. They knew that there were things that the squire would never tolerate, but that his attorney might attempt. True, it was said that, impossible as it might sound, Miss Psyche would help to look after the estate. But they expected from her no softness. Hence their sorrow at the owner's departure was genuine and sincere.

Psyche had wept much in secret, though not given usually to weeping, during the last few weeks. This morning, she was resolved, her eyes should be dry, her voice unbroken, as she took leave of the man and the child that she loved. She would not distress the squire with any maudlin exhibition of sorrow. But her heart was heavy as lead, and she felt that her world was falling to pieces about her.

'Where is Miss Psyche?' he asked of the young woman who carried in her arms the little girl carefully wrapped in a shawl as protection against the chilly morning air. Nurse and child were to travel in the buggy to Kingston along with him.

'In there, massa,' answered the girl, pointing to the sitting-room. 'Miss Psyche tell me to tell you she waitin' to tell y'u goodbye, sah.'

Psyche was standing in the lighted sitting-room, which hardly was ever used; she was neatly dressed in white. She lifted her eyes as the squire came into the room; she had seen him but ten minutes before, had superintended his final packing, and then had slipped away, for she wanted her leave-taking to be unwitnessed by other people. In those few minutes a change had swept over her countenance. Huntingdon, sad at heart himself, was startled. Wretchedness stared out of her eyes.

'Aren't you coming outside to see us off, Psyche?' he asked.

'Yes, Squire, but I wanted to bid you goodbye alone, and to ask you one last favour.'

She paused, but he saw that she had more to say, so he waited silently.

'Squire,' she resumed, 'you know, after little Psyche was born I used to think that nothing bad could ever happen to me again. I was so happy.'

He had nothing to say in reply: what could he say? Presently she continued.

'Long, long ago, they took me from my village in Africa. I was frightened then, but I was young, and on the slave-ship the captain treated me well.

'Then I came to Jamaica, and you bought me. And you have been good to me—ever so good. You have been like your God.'

'You mustn't say that, Psyche!' he ejaculated; 'I am afraid that at times I have been very selfish.'

'No. Not even when Miss Josephine Brookfield tried to take you away from me. For, after all, she was young and pretty and white, and any man would have done what you did. But even then, Squire, you liked me better than she. I know that.

'Then she died—suddenly. You were sorry, Squire, and yet not sorry—you understand what I mean. You came back to me, and from that time to this you have stuck to me alone. No other man in this country would have done it. I want to thank you for that, Squire. On my knees.'

She sank to her knees; he seized her by the shoulders. 'Get up, Psyche,' he cried. 'You must not kneel to any-one. But I thank you for what you have said—from my heart.'

'I have been happy, too happy all this time, Squire,' she continued, as she rose under his compelling gesture. 'Do you think, Squire, that it is because I have been too happy that I must pay for it now?'

'Where did you learn that doctrine, girl?' he asked wonderingly. 'Why, it is Greek. The gods, the old Greeks used to say, grow jealous of a mortal's too great happiness. But you can know nothing of such philosophy. How could you know of it?'

'We all know it, Squire. The slaves here always say that "when chicken merry, hawk is going to catch him". Isn't that what you mean?'

'Yes, I suppose it amounts to the same thing. Strange that I have never heard that Negro proverb before.'

'It is true; I was very merry, and I didn't see the hawk. It has caught me.

'I am losing everything now that I love: you, the child. And I must leave the Great House tomorrow. Not that I mind that,' she hastened to add; 'I wouldn't stay here for anything without you; I prefer the little house on my own property. But I see now that it is not good to be too happy and to believe that nothing bad can ever happen to you. Yet, Squire, I want little Psyche to be happy. Perhaps there will be no hawk for her.'

'I have promised to do my best for the child,' he returned. 'Surely you do not doubt me, Psyche?'

'No, Squire, nobody who knows you will ever doubt you. You will put little Psyche to school in your own country, you say, and will bring her up as a white girl: as a white girl in a white country. And you will see that she doesn't want for anything, and I will see to that, too. Already I am not poor, and I will stint myself for her.'

'There will be no need for you to do that, Psyche. I am rich now, and even were I poor I should work for my own flesh and blood.'

'Yes, Squire; I know you would; but I will work too, so that my daughter shall grow up wealthy and be a lady. And this is what I am going to beg of you. If when she is growing big she remembers me and asks after me, tell her I was her nurse. Never tell her I am her mother!'

'But, Psyche——'

'You yourself said, Squire, when you told me that you wanted to take her to England with you, that she might not wish to come back here. I have been thinking about that for a long time. You were right; but if she knows that her mother is out here and still alive—don't you see? She may want to come back on a visit, and then she will learn too much. But if you tell her that her nurse is in Jamaica—

and I have been her nurse as well as her mother—and that her mother was a lady and is dead, she will feel different. She won't want to come back. . . . So promise me, Squire.'

'I promise,' he said, 'but don't think that you are the only one that feels this parting.'

He added, 'Isn't it terrible for you to cut yourself off from everything like this—from your own child?'

'No. It is best for her, and that will make me as happy as I am likely to be now.'

'You have more strength of character, and more intelligence than any other woman I have ever met,' he said sadly. 'I don't think that I have ever known you well, Psyche. I seem to have realised only a part of you.'

She smiled slightly at these words. No: he had not known her very well, after all. Had never guessed her thoughts, probed her ambitions. He had never known either that she had deliberately killed Josephine Brookfield and had never regretted that act, though they called it murder in this country and punished it with death. She would kill again, if necessary, though now it would not be for herself, but would be for her child or for him. She would kill as a duty, be merciless, dealing death so that good might come of it. For that was the creed in which she believed.

But had good really come of her poisoning Josephine? Had she herself ultimately benefited by that? She had had some years of happiness; but would not all her future now be lonely and bitter, cut off as she would be from everything that she held dear and that she had never thought to lose? She had won much; now she was about to begin to pay the price for all that she had won. She was losing all. Everything was disappearing, as the mist rising from the river would presently disappear when smitten by the rays of the risen sun.

But the child would never know of the circumstances of her early life; the child would be happier than she. And the child's future was more than worth the mother's future or past.

So she thought, and in that thought she found some consolation.

'It's time you started, Squire,' she said at length. 'You have a long journey before you.'

A shout of welcome greeted his presence when he appeared on the front steps of the Great House; the slaves pressed round him; most of them, with the undisciplined emotion of the untutored African, openly weeping. Behind him, almost unnoticed, Psyche stood, but she fought back her tears and tried to smile. Mrs. Buxton was there too, and her husband; their farewells were subdued; it seemed that they too were genuinely affected by this final taking of leave. Both of them felt that this was the last they would ever see of the master.

Huntingdon hurried into the buggy, where his child already was. Up to then little Psyche had been all excitement, thrilled with the idea of making her first long journey. But now it came to her that she was leaving her mother, and suddenly she held out her arms to Psyche, crying aloud. The memory of that mother would fade from her mind as the years went on; she would come to believe as she grew older that it was only a nurse that still lived in Jamaica, a nurse who had loved her and who was devoting her life to her. She would have a vague blurred memory of black faces, of waving green fields, of fierce sunlight, of brilliant blue skies. England to her would be home; Jamaica merely the place where she was born. But now it was from a mother that she was going, and she felt frightened and sorrow-struck; and so she stretched out her arms and cried bitterly.

But Psyche had already kissed the child goodbye, and now she held herself away, not wishing to prolong the agony of that moment.

All her mother-instincts pulled her toward the little girl;

she fought them down. Nor did Charles Huntingdon turn his eyes to right or left once he had taken his seat in the carriage. He sat as though carved out of wood, a living statue in the surrounding dimness.

Then the driver shook his reins, cracked his whip, and the heavy conveyance lurched forward. Under the paling skies and amidst the shouts of the assembled people, Charles Huntingdon and his child rolled away from Hope Vale estate.

BOOK TWO

Chapter 13

THE LETTER

'FOREVER.'

The word hummed in the brain of the woman whose fingers held the letter she had received but half an hour before, a letter posted weeks ago in England and written in a handwriting indicating a disposition strong and firm, immovable, a character resolute and also imperious.

The woman who had received and read the letter over and over again sat at the threshold of a neat wooden house built upon a knoll and overlooking cattle pastures each neatly separated from the others by stone hedges; in these pastures strolled or stood ruminating cattle chewing their cud. Some were lying down; all appeared in excellent condition; while the slave-workers who looked after the beasts moved about nimble and alert.

She was gazing, not at the things that stirred or stood before her eyes, but at vacancy; her eyes were fixed and still, in them was a look that spoke poignantly of agony of heart. Her lips moved slightly; ears that were acute might have caught the word they uttered again and again— 'forever, forever, forever'. It was a word she had repeated with mingled sorrow and relief over twenty years ago when the man and the child she had borne to him, and both of whom she loved dearer than life, had left Jamaica for England: sorrow, because she had believed that never again would she see them; relief, because, though her heart was torn, she preferred for her child's sake that they should be eternally separated. But now the letter she held in her hand told her that her former master was dead; the man who had had no other children and whose title of baron had now gone to a distant relative, with the property in England which was entailed, had passed away at last.

But her daughter, her little Psyche—for always she thought of the girl as a child—had easily won her way upward in the world. For some time this woman had known that the girl had married a Frenchman, a Baron de Brion, who had died two years ago but had left a son who bore his father's title. Baron de Brion, a scion of the old noblesse of France, had been a poor man, but his wife had been very well-off. All the money that her father had saved had been bestowed upon her year after year; all the money earned by the Jamaica property of Hope Vale in St. James had also been invested for Lord Huntingdon's daughter, and now Hope Vale itself was hers. And her mother's cattle property, which had done so well—most of the revenue from that had gone to little Psyche too, and the place itself would be hers some day, though of mother and of cattle-pen care was taken that she should know nothing. But did she need to come back to Jamaica to see these properties, thought the older woman, when they were so properly looked after and some good attorney for them would be found in the days to come? To return to Jamaica now or in the future would mean surely that Psyche would learn the truth about herself, learn she was a coloured woman, might even be told that the woman with aquiline features and straight hair, though black complexion—was her mother. The fates had played a scurvy trick on one who had dared to trust them much.

On his return to England years ago, because of his elder brother's death, Charles Huntingdon had married as a matter of duty, to produce an heir to the title and the great property he had inherited. But after several years he felt that his sickly wife would never bear a child; and when she died he did not marry again. He had no wish to; he felt he had fully done his duty; besides, his mother, too, who had wanted to see an heir of her own blood, was also dead. Little Psyche, who was very nearly seven years of age when she reached England, had been boarded in excellent schools, and soon began growing into a fine girl; during the last three years of his wife's life she had spent her holidays with her father and his wife at the castle in which they lived. Psyche passed as his niece. She called him uncle; his wife she had learnt to call aunt, though Lady Hunting-don knew well that Psyche was her husband's daughter. But she grew to like the girl more and more, and never would she allude to her birth on a Jamaica slave estate; as to the scholars and teachers in the schools which Psyche attended—and her father took care that these institutions should be of the best—they regarded her complexion as a result of a West Indian climate, especially as her hair was soft and long, a heritage from her maternal Arab great-grandfather as well as from her father, and thought principally about her connection with the old nobility of England. It was imagined that a brother of Lord Hunting-don had been with him, or before him, in the West Indies, and that Psyche was his orphan daughter. In time, in a vague sort of way, Psyche came to believe this herself; there was nothing to awaken in her a memory of the past. Then at seventeen she went to France with a chaperon carefully selected by her father, and at eighteen she married Gustave de Brion, who was nearly twice her age. Her father fully approved. Gustave boasted of as proud a descent as any Huntingdon. And if, as a result of the comparatively recent French Revolution, he was poor, Psyche at least was wealthy, and so about material financial cares they had nothing whatever to worry.

Psyche cared for her husband, but never passionately loved him. He was kind, considerate, honourable; when they were in England they lived with her father, who had now his daughter alone to cherish, and then her boy when it was born. Occasionally she and her husband went to Lon-don, but she preferred rural England, sharing in this the tastes both of her father and husband. Her son, who de

Brion thought was the image of his ancestors, while Huntingdon secretly was satisfied that the youngster was every
inch a Huntingdon, was three years of age when his father
died, in France, and two years after Lord Huntingdon was
also dead. This was in 1831. It was then that the Baroness
de Brion came to a resolution which she might never have
seriously entertained but for this double bereavement, this
sundering of the ties that bound her to the English life she
so much loved.

She would visit her estate in Jamaica, go for a short
sojourn in the country where she was born. She remembered
hardly anything of it, knew only of one old woman—she
thought of her as old—who when she was a little child had
been her nurse, and still wrote to her occasionally as 'Miss
Psyche'; but she knew she would not even recognise this
woman should she meet her suddenly. It seemed to her
amusing that this woman's name should also be Psyche, that
she had now to be addressed as Psyche Huntingdon. But
slaves, even those manumitted, usually took the names of
their masters, her father had told her. She thought this a
wise custom: it must help to bind masters and people
together, she reflected sometimes.

And now her letter was in her 'nurse's' hand, and the set,
somewhat stern face looked as though it were scanning a
future that held unimaginable bitterness for so many
unsuspecting persons.

Not far from her an old man sat on a box shelling a small
heap of Indian corn placed beside him, the ripe grains of
which fell into the great calabash that lay between his feet.
His head was white, his movements slow, he seemed to be
eighty years of age or more; yet his eyes were alert, as was
evidenced by the keen glances that he shot at his mistress
from time to time. Noticing the continued motionlessness
of her form, rightly connecting her stricken appearance with
the letter that had been brought from Montego Bay but
half an hour ago, he now rose and walked over to her,

displaying as he did so a figure which must once have been
gigantic but was now shrunken with age. 'What's the
matter, Miss Psyche?' he murmured. 'Bad news?'

'She's coming back, Mashimba,' she answered; then
ceased as though she had said enough.

'Coming here, Miss Psyche?'

'Yes.'

'When?'

He could not read, so she did not hand him the letter;
mechanically she replied: 'She say here she will start in the
next ship, so she must already be on the way. She may be
here four weeks' time. Only God can tell.'

'I thoughted she went away forever when she was a baby,
like her fader. I long night an' day to see her sweet face
again, Miss Psyche; but yet . . .'

'I understand, Mashimba; but what we going to do now?
What we going to do?'

She was the only one on the property to call him in these
days by his old African name. To everyone else he was
Homer. The woman, Miss Psyche, had made him free when
he was seventy-two years of age, and after he had been some
twenty years in Jamaica. Mashimba had a son now, too,
a young fellow over twenty years of age. This young man
had already succeeded to his position on the property; in
reality if not in appearance, under Psyche Huntingdon he
was the real boss of the place which produced some of the
finest cattle in St. James parish with a surprisingly small
number of slaves.

Mashimba stood looking down upon his mistress thoughtfully; they had spoken without mentioning any name but
both knew to whom they referred. So 'she' was coming back
to the land in which she had been born, ruminated Mashimba; and though she must have forgotten almost everything
in the years that had elapsed since she went away, might
she not remember, or more probably be reminded of,
something connected with her past on her return? That, he

knew, was what her mother feared: that was what must be prevented. Such prevention surely was not hard if they spoke to the older slaves on this little cattle farm, Cowbend, and also to the people on the neighbouring property of Hope Vale, at once. Mashimba voiced his view.

'Nobody mus' tell her anything, Miss Psyche. You mus' warn them.'

'Warn nigger people, Mashimba?' she replied bitterly. 'You think them will care?'

'Ef them doan't we can tell them we will beat hell out a dem,' said the old man dispassionately, and anyone who knew him would have known that he meant what he said and that, under some pretext or other, his son would inflict terrific punishment on any slave who dared to disobey this most sacred injunction.

'Very well,' agreed Psyche Huntingdon, resignedly, seeing that the old man's plan was the only one to be adopted. 'I will speak to Mr. Buxton about it. I will go over to Hope Vale now.'

They brought her a horse, and she rode over to Hope Vale. Mr. Buxton, its co-manager and attorney, was still alive, but was now past sixty-five years of age. His hair was white, his face wrinkled, yet he seemed far more at peace with himself and with the world than when Psyche had first known him as overseer of Hope Vale. Even when his wife was still alive, Psyche and he had managed the affairs of the estate together as co-attorneys.

From the beginning the arrangement had worked exceedingly well. Psyche took care only to make suggestions to Mr. Buxton: the actual orders were given to the estate workers and others by him. She openly interfered in no way with managing the estate, but Mr. Buxton realised that she understood many matters that might have been a mystery to a woman of lesser intelligence, and this caused him to be careful not to follow in the footsteps of the average Jamaica estate attorney, who specialised in knavery.

Buxton had an excellent job, and knew it. He stood more to lose than to gain by dishonesty at Hope Vale.

It was about a year after Mr. Huntingdon's departure from Hope Vale that Mrs. Buxton found that she was about to become a mother. She was rather old for that, she felt, and in her heart was the fear that she might die. Who too was to help her in her coming time of trouble: the ordinary Jamaica midwife whose ministrations she dreaded; the doctor at Montego Bay who might come to see her when it was too late? To her astonishment Psyche Huntingdon offered her services, and Mrs. Buxton was equally astonished when she heard herself accepting them. Yet she was glad she had done so, for she found Psyche attentive, solicitous of her comfort, anxious for her welfare. She doubted now whether she had not been altogether wrong in thinking that the young woman had had anything to do with Josephine Brookfield's death!

When the baby was born, it proved a healthy boy, but Mrs. Buxton's premonitions as to her own fate were justified. The Montego Bay doctor told Mr. Buxton bluntly that his wife was dying; told Psyche also, though Psyche, who had helped many a slave woman quietly through her time of tribulation, had already guessed that. And Mrs. Buxton knew it; indeed, it was not difficult for her to read the terror-stricken look on her husband's face. She called Psyche to her bedside when they were left alone and, pointing to the baby, begged her in a weak voice to 'look after him when I am gone'. The young woman bowed her head and promised. That promise she never forgot.

Young Buxton was about twenty-one years of age now, the age of Mashimba's son. He would succeed his father as manager of Hope Vale; his capabilities no one could doubt. Mashimba's boy, who had been named Charles after Mr. Huntingdon, would assist him: all his life he had been devoted to Marse Edward, who in fact, when he was fifteen, had strongly argued with Psyche and Mashimba that

Charles should never have been allowed to remain so many years a slave. Mashimba could well afford to buy his freedom, but simply had never thought of doing so; Psyche could make him free without receiving a penny of compensation. Both, argued young Edward Buxton, had shamefully neglected their duty. They hastened to agree. So Mashimba's son, named Charles Huntingdon, had been a free man for at least six years of his life. And what Marse Edward Buxton said to him was law.

Psyche rode up to the office of the manager, and was lucky to find him in. He nodded her to a chair, smiled:

'What is it now, Psyche?' he enquired.

She handed him the letter: 'She coming back to Jamaica, to Hope Vale, Marse Joe,' she replied laconically.

Like Mashimba, he knew at once whom she meant. None of the three ever spoke of the Baroness de Brion but as 'she': it was a habit. Mr. Buxton knew, also, that the baroness was now the mistress of Hope Vale; her father's will made her that, the laws of England, supporting the will, made her that, and the new Jamaica laws, passed only in the previous year, made her that also. There could be no disputing her rights. And no one was inclined to dispute them.

'She start already,' continued Psyche. 'She'll be here three—four weeks' time.'

Mr. Buxton nodded. 'You going to tell her anything?'

'No, Marse Joe, we mustn't.'

'You right, Psyche; you must talk to the people on Cowbend, an' I will talk to those here. Not many of the old ones alive now,' he continued reflectively. 'Some dead, some gone to other properties; but some remain and the younger ones must have heard something. I will talk to everyone of them, and they better mind what I say! I am not making any fun!'

Neither the white man nor the black woman was aware that they spoke somewhat differently now from how they spoke when Mr. Charles Huntingdon lived at Hope Vale; that they were slipping more and more into the Negro drawl and dialect which slaves, free people and whites not of the best educated classes, commonly used in Jamaica. Indeed, they still spoke in better fashion than their neighbours and those by whom they were surrounded; yet the falling off, the vocal degeneracy, could not possibly be denied. Neither minded it, was aware of it. It seemed to them more normal, more natural, than any different fashion of speech.

'You mus' do you' best, Marse Joe, an' I will do mine,' said Psyche. 'We can't do better. Where is she to stay, Marse Joe?'

'In the Great House where I live now, of course; it is hers, you know. I will begin to move out from today, and get it fix up. She'll be lonely, Psyche.'

'No white lady goin' to come an' see her,' agreed Psyche bitterly. 'My God, why did she make up her mind to come back!'

'They can all go to hell,' cried Mr. Buxton savagely. 'Her 'usband was a nobleman, wasn't he, an' her father was one. Why should she care what a lot of bastards do?'

'*She* is the bastard, Marse Joe, not they: you forget that?'

'But she don't know, so what does it matter?' he demanded illogically. 'Well, I'm a white man, and they will all see how I respect her. How many men in this country work first under a lord, and then under his daughter, a baroness? Not one except me! I am better than all o' them, and me son is strong enough to kick any s—— of a b—— that say a word about me I don't like. Don't worry, Psyche: we'll fix everything, you and me, like we always do.'

'Thank you, Marse Joe: goodbye.'

'Goodbye; an' remember me son will kick to hell anyone who is forward enough to forget themself.'

Chapter 14

HOMECOMING

THE tall slim young woman, golden-coloured, aristocratic in appearance, simple in demeanour, yet with a touch of hauteur of which she herself was unconscious, stood on the topmost tread of the flight of steps leading up to the front entrance of the Hope Vale Great House.

She had arrived the evening before from Falmouth, having stopped for some hours in that town previously to taking the last lap of her journey from Kingston to her property in St. James. All the arrangements for her lodging in the towns through which they had passed had long since been made by Edward Buxton, who had been sent by his father to Kingston to meet the mistress of Hope Vale. Edward had taken Charles, Mashimba's son, with him; and both these young men had made it a point to speak of the baroness as though she were first cousin to the King of England himself! This had its intended effect on the obsequious proprietors of the Jamaica Inns, or Taverns as they were called.

She had arrived fairly late at Hope Vale the evening before, and as there was then no moon had seen nothing of the property. This morning her employees and slaves were all assembled before the Great House to bid her welcome. She too wanted to convey a word of cheer to them.

'Am I supposed to make a speech?' she laughingly enquired of Mr. Buxton, who stood on a step lower than hers on the flight from which much of the property could be overlooked.

'Not unless your ladyship wants,' he answered. 'Do you wish to make a speech?'

'Certainly not,' she laughed, 'if it is not the custom—and I am glad it isn't. But you may tell them for me, Mr. Buxton, how glad I am to be here, and to see them. They all look well,' she added: 'evidently you have treated them well. For that I must thank you.'

He shouted her greeting loudly; there was no one there who did not hear it. A chorus of cries welcomed it: 'T'ank you, missis; God bless you, ma'am; we very glad to see you.'

Buxton's sharp eyes were everywhere. His ears were on the alert. Evidently the warning he had given slaves and hired people alike had had its effect. As he had added that he would half-murder anyone who disregarded his warning, while his son stood prepared to kick savagely any person whatever who forgot himself in dealing with the baroness, it may be assumed that fear as much as respect played its part in this vociferous welcome accorded to the Baroness de Brion.

'But my old nurse, Mr. Buxton; I do not see her,' said the baroness. 'Surely she should have been on these steps with us?'

'She refused to come up till she was asked by yourself, Baroness. There she is.'

He pointed to where Psyche stood in the front of the crowd below, her face like a mask, her arms quietly folded across her stomach.

The baroness did not recognise her; it was a stranger she saw standing there. But she remembered all that her father had told her about the kindness, the loving care of this woman; she knew too that Psyche held with Mr. Buxton equal powers of attorney on Hope Vale property. Before Mr. Buxton could beckon Psyche to join them, the baroness had run down the steps and clasped her old nurse to her heart. 'Thank God,' broke from the lips of a very old man who stood near to Psyche Huntingdon, but so low was the voice of Mashimba that few could hear his words. 'Nurse,'

cried the baroness, 'I have looked forward for years to this
day. I cannot adequately thank you for all you did for me
when I was but a baby.'

Psyche curtsied low, successfully fighting back her tears.
But the Negro is emotional, and almost everyone in that
crowd knew of the real relationship in which the two women
stood. Some were weeping silently; the lips of others moved
as though in prayer. Mr. Buxton's eyes rolled about fiercely,
compelling reticence and a comparative calm. Yet his own
eyes were glistening, though he would have cursed anyone
who had dared to suggest that he himself was not very far
from tears.

The black woman, not yet fifty, gazed upon the countenance of the lady who stood before her, and saw only in her
golden complexion any sign of the blood which the Baroness
de Brion had inherited from her. The lady was unmistak-
ably Huntingdon, yet had not the softness, almost the
melancholy, of her father. She had thrown back to an
earlier generation of her father's people, looked indubitably
the scion of a family accustomed to rule, to be obeyed, to
be treated with deference, to command respect.

Of medium height, she was still slim in figure though
now approaching thirty years of age. Indeed, because of the
climate and of the easy circumstances in which she had
been brought up, she looked but twenty-five at most; in
appearance she was still girlish, her complexion much
lighter than it would have been had she passed all the
earlier period of her life completely under the Jamaica
sun. Dark, widely spaced eyes looked at you frankly from
beneath a broad brow expressive of candour; there was
pride in those eyes but they also seemed capable of express-
ing intense affection. She wore her hair looped over her
ears and coiled in a great knot at the nape of her neck; her
nose was not aquiline like her mother's, but straight with
sensitive nostrils, as her father's had been; it was the
Huntingdon nose. Yet it might have been somewhat

platerine had not her mother inherited her Arab grandfather's aquiline features; these were too pronounced in
the older woman not to have influenced somewhat the
face-formation of her daughter.

The lips were full, but not in the least sensual; the upper
lip a trifle too long. A glance at it and the reader of
physiognomy would have said at once that this young
woman possessed a strong will and might even be un-
reasonably stubborn upon occasion. Yet the face was a
prepossessing, even a very handsome one, and there were
times when its expression could soften wonderfully. There
were also times, however, when it could harden like steel,
and then it was that the resemblance of the baroness to her
African mother would suddenly flash out conspicuously,
though as yet there had been no one to notice that; then it
could be seen, as in a revelation, that this young woman
might ruthlessly be cruel as death.

Small feet, long, beautiful hands; one observed these at
once; but her mother had no eyes now but for the face of her
beloved. She could have knelt to her and worshipped her.
Never had she imagined that her daughter would grow
into the great lady she saw standing before her, with a look
and carriage which bespoke one born to command and
never to think disobedience possible.

'Come inside the house with me, nurse; surely we have
many things to talk about,' said Lady de Brion, taking
Psyche by the hand and leading her.

'Yes, ma'am,' meekly replied Psyche, all obedience and
controlled emotion now.

She and her daughter passed within the doors of the
front veranda of the Great House; the assembly outside
broke up. 'Now let us have a long talk, nurse,' said the
baroness, glancing keenly at the face of the middle-aged
woman who sat stiffly in a chair opposite to her.

She saw at once that this woman, still under fifty years
of age, was handsome yet and carried herself as one far,

far removed from the status of a slave. She noticed that Psyche's hair, now growing grey, was long and straight, her features aquiline. 'A superior type,' she thought; 'not like anyone else I have seen on this estate.'

'You know, nurse,' she began, 'that I imagined this place to be immense, and that you had hundreds of slaves here. My old childish imagination, of course.'

'We had more slaves once, Miss Psyche; but I think Mr. Buxton wrote to tell you' uncle after the war was over that he was turning Hope Vale partly into a cattle property, as cattle would pay better than sugar. We don't make half the sugar now like we did fifteen years ago and the prices gone to nothing. But our rum'—Psyche spoke proudly—'is the best in this parish, an' we get a good price for it. And our cattle sell well.'

'You and Mr. Buxton have done wonders for my uncle and me,' said the baroness; 'I cannot be sufficiently grateful. The slaves here seem happy enough, too—happy as slaves can ever be. I suppose most of them will be willing to work for wages when emancipation comes?'

'Emancipation? You don't believe that that is coming, me lady?'

'Oh, but it is; slavery can last but a little while longer now, nurse.'

'But that will ruin us!' cried the elder woman. 'We buy the slaves an' the British Government take them away for nothing and make them free!'

'My uncle always said that there should never have been any slaves, and I think he is right. Maybe I will set my own people here free before returning to England—we shall see. I believe—I think my uncle told me—that his brother, my father, and my mother also, hated slavery. By the way, both of them died in Jamaica and were buried here. You know where, of course?'

Psyche Huntingdon's face grew grey as she heard this question; it was one that she had feared for weeks. But she had prepared her answer and she gave it unfalteringly. She thought it would pass.

'I wasn't at their funeral, Miss Psyche; they died far away from Hope Vale, in a parish called St. Andrew. I think they are buried in the burying ground of the St. Andrew Parish Church, but am not quite sure. It is a long time now.'

'Yes, I suppose so. Well, if I ever go to this St. Andrew place I must look up the graves of my parents—I don't remember them. You yourself have a small cattle pen near here, haven't you? Mr. Buxton told me so last night.'

'Yes, miss. You must come an' see it some day.'

'I'll come this afternoon; I'll ride over with Mr. Buxton. And if you want anything . . ?'

'Nothing, miss; I have everything I want.'

'That's what everybody on this property says to whom I have spoken,' laughed the baroness. 'You know, nurse, I don't quite like it! I think that such general contentment —if it is sincere—is unlucky. So much happiness, if it really exists, cannot last and must be paid for.

'My uncle,' she continued, 'used to tell me that once you repeated to him an old Jamaica proverb, which I remember clearly still. It was that "when chicken is merry, hawk is going to catch him". It is true. But what hawk can possibly be threatening Hope Vale and its people now?'

Psyche Huntingdon did not answer, but was conscious of a sinking, sickening sensation at the pit of her stomach. She knew that hawks, invisible, were hovering over Hope Vale even now; she did not believe that, take all the precautions they might, they could prevent one of these creatures from swooping to the attack, with disastrous consequences to the mistress, and possibly to the people, of Hope Vale. Well, what was to come must come, and as she thought this there glowed in her eyes a look which, years before her daughter was born, Josephine Brookfield might have seen had she been attentive, and so, possibly, might have saved her life. She stood up suddenly. 'You will ride over to Cowbend this evening, miss?'

'Yes; when the sun is going down. In these months it sets early, I believe.'

'Yes, miss. From now on—this is the beginning of October—it will be darker and darker every afternoon till April. Darker and darker,' she repeated, as though the words had for her some hidden significance and meaning.

'Well, goodbye until later on, nurse. By the way, I don't think you have yet met my maid: she will go back with me to England in February. Gladys!'

The maid came at the call, a practical, intelligent-looking Englishwoman of about thirty-two. She had been with the baroness for many years now, and although she had not liked the notion of travelling to Jamaica, which she freely spoke of as 'a nigger country', she had followed her mistress thither when she had perceived that the latter was determined to make the journey.

'Gladys, this is my old nurse; you have often heard me speak of her in England?'

Gladys bowed politely, so did Psyche Huntingdon, who then turned quickly away. Secretly Gladys thought of Psyche as 'a terrible old woman'. She could not have explained why she had that feeling.

And that afternoon the baroness rode over to Cowbend with Mr. Buxton. She was charmed with the neatness, the order, the efficiency she observed. She met old Mashimba, who spoke vaguely—he had been instructed so to speak—of her father and mother who lay buried so far away in another part of the island, and who quite naturally talked about Hope Vale and Cowbend as though they were his own properties. Then Psyche Huntingdon walked with them towards a gate of Cowbend through which they might easily ride to Hope Vale.

At that moment she observed a wild flutter among some

chickens near at hand that were just going to roost; she turned her head upwards and perceived a hawk darting swiftly down towards them.

'Already,' she muttered bitterly. She saw an omen of dread significance in a simple, ordinary fact.

Chapter 15

REALISATIONS

MRS. BENEDICT was puzzled. Also worried. Her husband pretended indifference, which he did not really feel; his brother registered impudence and insolence which came quite naturally to him. This early morning they were awaiting a business visitor. Mr. and Mrs. Benedict sincerely wished that it were someone else.

'They say, Rupert, that she is prepared to pay more for this property than anybody else. I suppose that is true?' commented Mrs. Benedict anxiously.

'You have said that a dozen times already,' replied her husband testily. 'You know that I have two offers already. Do you imagine I would sell her Creighton for the same price I would take from a white person?'

'Naturally not,' exclaimed his brother, who sat jacketless, with feet elevated on the round mahogany table which was the chief piece of furniture in the little sitting-room. 'We have come to a fine pitch as it is with these mulatto people being able to buy property! And now the law is that they can vote and shall have all the rights and privileges of white people. What next I wonder!'

'And she doesn't seem to know who she really is,' suggested Mrs. Benedict. 'I hear she carries on as if she was a lady, and calls her mother "nurse". When she finds out——'

'I think I will tell her the truth today,' growled Arthur Benedict savagely. 'After she has arranged about Creighton, of course.'

'You won't do it here, Arthur,' asseverated his married brother firmly, while Mrs. Benedict looked startled. 'It is none of our business, and she might back out of buying

Creighton after you had been rude to her. You just keep your mouth shut.'

'That's she coming now,' exclaimed Mrs. Benedict, heart-glad to change a topic that might lead to a nasty row. All three of them ran to an open window to watch the small cavalcade as it moved towards the house.

Mr. Buxton came first, leading the way, and then the baroness. After her rode Mr. Buxton's son, alongside of the heir of Mashimba. Creighton was a cattle pen; it bordered Hope Vale on the south. It was not a very large place or particularly successful. It lacked the careful management that had made Cowbend so prosperous a property so far; yet it had not fallen into bankruptcy, and Benedict was selling it only because a relative of his had left him a fair estate in the south-east of the island upon which he must live if he hoped to make money out of it. In St. Thomas-in-the-East he might become almost a considerable planter; in St. James he was but a middling white landowner who was patronised by the other white planters of the district and never for one moment regarded as their equal.

News that he wished to dispose of Creighton had got about; offers had been made for the property, but they were not very liberal. Then Benedict had been informed that the proprietress of Hope Vale wanted to add Creighton to Hope Vale and that she would ride over on a certain morning to make an offer for the place. Mr. Buxton had suggested that Lady de Brion would pay more for Creighton than anybody else; as a matter of fact it was on his suggestion and that of Psyche that Creighton was being acquired.

For Mr. Buxton had long since realised, and had also brought Psyche Huntingdon to see, that the days of huge prices for sugar were passed and over and that the money Hope Vale had made during the Napoleonic Wars would never be made again. Cattle, on the other hand, could thrive in this district, were sparsely bred on the whole, and

were always in demand for beef and also for heavy transportation purposes. Buxton's advice, and Psyche's, had
determined the baroness to purchase Creighton if the price
were reasonable; it would be amusing to do something in
the way of business during her sojourn in the island. Hence
her journey of this morning. It was just three weeks after
she had arrived at Hope Vale.

At the end of that time an observer who had known her
previously would have noticed an almost perpetual frown
upon her brow. Little hints, suggestions, furtive looks,
expressions that seemed to hold a double meaning, coming
from some of the older people on Hope Vale, had caused
her to think furiously, to suspect much, during the past
fortnight; but most of all the contributory influences to her
dawning realisation that hers was a peculiar position was
the marked absence of any caller whatever at Hope Vale.
She knew, for she had been told, that after a new proprietor
had been established in his property for a week or less, men
and women would come flocking to pay their regards; in
her case not a single person had made his appearance.
She had gone riding outside Hope Vale; she had occasionally met some of the local gentry on horseback or in the
vehicles then used for country drives. They must have
known who she was, but they kept their eyes averted; they
pretended not to be aware of her proximity. This had
happened again and again. She could have no doubt about
it now.

Hence in the last week or so her mien had become
haughtier than it hitherto had been, and anyone staring into
her dark eyes would have observed in them a smouldering
fire indicating that within this woman's breast a volcano
of anger and wrath was flaming and might erupt some day.
She also talked much less now than had been her custom
in the first week of her visit to Hope Vale; her lips were
firmly pressed together as a rule in these days. Psyche
noticed these symptoms, and was afraid. 'Trouble is

coming,' she whispered once to Mr. Buxton, and Buxton sorrowfully nodded his head in agreement.

The visitors arrived at the Creighton home; they dismounted; they entered the living-room of the house.

'The Baroness de Brion,' announced Mr. Buxton with a flourish, addressing Mr. and Mrs. Benedict; he took no notice whatever of Mr. Arthur Benedict; he knew too well that gentleman's reputation for rudeness.

The baroness extended her hand with a smile to Mrs. Benedict, who was secretly overawed by the title she had just heard announced with every indication of authenticity; to the two men she bowed slightly. Three pairs of eyes scrutinised her riding habit and noticed the perfect fit of it. The ample skirt was buff in colour; the jacket was scarlet, slightly open in front at the neck; a broad waist-band, riding gauntlets, knee-boots of polished black leather, a supple whip carried in the right hand completed the costume of the lady to whom Arthur Benedict wished to be rude but dared not be at the moment. Everyone realised that these riding accoutrements were expensive and guessed that they represented the last word of English fashion. Arthur felt that it was nothing short of immoral that a woman not ostensibly white should be so adorned. Had she been the mistress of some important planter, that of course, would have excused much and would certainly not have been immoral from any rational point of view. From which we may conclude that immorality depends upon one's point of view.

The baroness seated herself and glanced at Mrs. Benedict as if expecting her to do likewise; then her eyes suddenly lighted upon a rough shelf to her right which was crowded with books, and she was up again, gaily and eagerly this time, walking quickly over to the shelf to inspect the volumes there set out, tomes which obviously were in use and were not displayed merely for the purposes of ornament or ostentation.

She saw Shakespeare and Milton and Dryden; among the more modern poets she noticed Shelley and Wordsworth; there was also many another author with whose works she was well acquainted. She turned with a smile to Mrs. Benedict.

'These books are yours?'

Mrs. Benedict, a woman not older than thirty-five, had once been pretty and even now retained traces of her former looks. She had always been a timid creature, feeling herself infinitely superior to the coloured people of the country but also infinitely inferior to the white magnates of the land. These, she knew, secretly despised poetry and belles lettres of any sort; at any rate, those of them that cared for such things kept their preference secret as though it were something to be ashamed of. She herself read nothing, but her husband loved books. She now blurted out in reply:

'No, ma'am; they belong to me husband.'

Arthur Benedict nearly had a fit. A white woman to address a coloured one as 'ma'am'! Was any such thing ever heard of in Jamaica before? Did this not portend the end of all established order and law, the very consummation of the earth and all that existed on it? 'And what is worse,' thought Arthur, 'is that this mulatto woman seems to take Alice's subservience for granted.' Surely something must be done about all this!

Lady de Brion turned to Mr. Benedict with a complimentary smile.

'I must congratulate you on your excellent taste in literature,' she said. 'Tell me, what is really your favourite play by Shakespeare?'

'*Antony and Cleopatra*, my lady,' he stammered; 'though I suppose I should say *Hamlet*.'

'And why should you?' she demanded warmly. 'Why disguise our real preferences? *Antony and Cleopatra* is also my favourite Shakespearean play; it is terrible but beautiful . . . haunting.

'But surely no man should allow himself to be so led and dominated by a woman as Antony was,' she went on. 'He sacrificed everything for her, lost all. He was a weakling, a boy, not a man, when she chose to exert her power over him. What a tragedy it all was!'

'But he did not really regret it,' Benedict pointed out eagerly. 'At the last he thought one kiss from her worth all that he had thrown away, though he knew and said that he had been the greatest prince of the world, the noblest, and had fallen from great heights because of her. You remember?'

'Only too well. But he did not play his part as a man should have done; where Cleopatra was concerned he was a weakling.

'But we are not come together to talk about poetry and plays, Mr. Benedict,' she continued. 'You want to sell Creighton. I will buy it if your price is reasonable, and you have already been told that I will pay more for it than you have hitherto been offered. Let us all sit down and talk the matter over.'

'Would four thousand pounds not be reasonable, Baroness?' asked Benedict, prepared to be beaten down a thousand pounds, in the normal Jamaica fashion.

'It isn't worth more than two thousand five hundred pounds,' rapped out Buxton aggressively, 'and nobody has yet offered you quite as much as that for it.'

'We can get four thousand,' broke in Arthur Benedict; 'it is only a matter of waiting a while.' His tone was challenging, his manner insolent.

The baroness glanced at him as though he were something just found under a huge stone in the garden, then turned her eyes away. 'I believe the place is worth three thousand pounds,' she said; 'at least, so I have been told on excellent authority'—which authority was Mr. Buxton himself. 'Suppose I give you three thousand two hundred pounds, Mr. Benedict: wouldn't that satisfy you?'

Benedict instinctively realised that the extra two hundred pounds had been added because of his love for literature which had won the admiration of this strange coloured woman, the like of whom he had never met before. Also because Lady de Brion disdained bartering. He knew instinctively that he must now accept or refuse that offer definitely: that the deal must now be closed one way or the other or would be considered off.

'Very well, Lady de Brion,' he answered quietly.

'But'—began Arthur Benedict, who chafed under a silence that seemed to be imposed upon him: he was permitted to get no farther.

'Please go outside and get the headmen to check up the cattle on Creighton, Arthur,' ordered his brother. 'There are not too many of them,' he added ruefully to the baroness.

Arthur was really a hanger-on upon his brother; therefore he knew when he must obey commands or risk being humiliated before all and sundry. He grunted disdainfully, but went out. Lady de Brion rose.

'Well, this business is now over except for the drawing up of papers and the making of transfers or whatever the lawyers call it. Mr. Buxton, I am sure you will help me by seeing to that.'

She was charming, thought Mr. Benedict, choosing to regard as a favour what she might have commanded as a duty from her principal employee. But she was in high good humour this morning; for once, outside her own property, she had been treated as she was accustomed to be treated, with a deference that was spontaneous, natural, and which seemed to have far more relation to her personality than to her money.

She put out her hand to Mrs. Benedict and then to that lady's husband; both shook it respectfully. 'I hope you will do well on your new property in St. Thomas,' she said, then sprang lightly, a born horsewoman, from the mounting block in front of the building on to her horse. 'Buxton,' she said, 'I am going to ride home alone by the main road; I know my way about these parts pretty well by this. You go with your son and with Charles.' She waited for no answer, but touched her mount lightly with her whip and rode off. Behind her four men and one woman bowed low.

She rode in the direction of Hope Vale, going at an easy pace; it was now October and the risen sun did not render riding unpleasant. She was thinking of the people she had just left; of Rupert Benedict's love for culture, of his wife's efforts to appear to be somebody—efforts which were forever failing—of his brother's rudeness and insolence. For she had clearly perceived Arthur's attitude, but had also noticed how his elder brother had squashed it decisively. That sufficed. Yet here again there was a something that puzzled her, or rather, worried her, for the stage of puzzlement was passing now.

She had looked into a mirror many times since she had been in Jamaica; she had marked the difference in complexion between herself and even such a person as poor Mrs. Benedict. True she was much fairer, lighter in hue than people of her degree of mixed blood in Jamaica. Her almost life-long residence in Europe, her sheltered life on board ship, where she had been so rarely exposed to the sun, her poise, the influence of her social circle in England, all had had its effect upon her. Yet every now and then in the past three weeks there had come to her some hint of a difference between her and the white women of the parish, and she had perceived that Mr. Buxton was always on his guard and that her old 'nurse', Psyche Huntingdon, wore increasingly a worried, harassed look that there was no mistaking.

'Psyche Huntingdon.' The Huntingdon she understood; many persons on the estate bore that name today. But Psyche? She herself had been christened Psyche too. Was that a mere coincidence, or was there a deeper relationship between the two names and the persons who bore them?

Once or twice she had caught on old Psyche's face a look that reminded her of her own expression at times. Was this old nurse of hers a former nurse only and nothing more?

The sound of a horse's hooves going at a smart trot came to her ears; she knew she would shortly be overtaken. That did not matter; she had been passed by many riders during the last three weeks; they had not seemed interested in her, and she had certainly not been interested in them. The sound became louder, clearer; presently a horseman swept past her, glanced in her direction then reined in his steed to a slower pace. He was garbed in riding clothes and wore as a protection against the sun a wide-brimmed slouch hat. This hat he lifted as he bowed, then fell into a rapid walk beside her. 'The Baroness de Brion, I am sure,' he said; 'may I introduce myself? I am one of your neighbours: Frederick O'Brian of Plimsole.'

'Irish?' she asked, smiling.

'On my father's side; my mother was English. But I am all Irish in my sympathies; Ireland has been badly treated by England these hundreds of years. My father——'

'Mr. O'Brian,' interrupted the baroness with a laugh that robbed her words of any suspicion of offence, 'please remember that my father's name was Huntingdon and that therefore all my sympathies are really with the English, my own people. So let us not talk politics. Plimsole is your property? I have passed it now and then.'

'You have to pass it when going to the Bay.'

'I hear it used to belong to some other people—I forget their name at the moment.'

'I have only owned it about fifteen years; my father got it for a debt, I believe, and left it to me.'

'Then you have been here fifteen years?'

'More or less. I went home some five years ago and remained for twelve months. I don't know when I shall go again. I have settled down now to become a regular Jamaica planter. Are you too here for good?'

'No; I should leave in February next or March at the latest,' she answered. 'I want to make some arrangements about my slaves before I go.'

'They seem to be well looked after. Buxton is a good man.'

'They are well looked after; but they won't remain slaves for very long now, you know. Emancipation is coming more quickly than people out here seem to believe.'

'Hum. You are sure of that?'

'Very. And surely it is right that the bondsmen should be set free. My uncle Charles—Lord Huntingdon, you know —was always of that opinion. Happily, his slaves had little or nothing to complain of.'

'Your uncle? O yes, of course.'

She looked at him searchingly: 'Why do you say that?'

'I? Nothing whatever. Of course I did not know your uncle.'

'But you must have heard of him, if not of my father, his younger brother, who died out here?'

'Yes, I have heard of him.'

To himself he thought: 'She has not yet learnt the truth about her parentage. But does she not suspect?' He decided to change the subject.

They were close to Hope Vale now; indeed, were at one of its gates. 'Will you let me ride with you to the Great House?' he asked, and she replied, 'With pleasure.'

She had been studying him as they rode along. A tall blue-eyed Irishman he looked; his reddish hair indicating quickness of temper, his laughing mouth a reckless, good-humoured disposition. He was not exactly handsome, but there was something frank, something winning about his countenance that made an instant appeal to her; she liked him at once. He appeared to be about thirty-seven years of age, and already about his temples the auburn hair was slightly streaked with grey.

They were at the Great House now; he sprang off his horse and held out his hand to help her down. She touched it lightly and easily dismounted: a woman well accustomed to horses, he immediately thought. 'Well, goodbye,' he said, 'and may I come to see you?'

'Whenever you like.'

'This afternoon?'

She laughed: 'If you care to so soon,' she answered.

'This afternoon, then; we should have much to talk about. You are from the old country, and you have suddenly made me feel like a stranger in Jamaica.'

'It is I who am the stranger,' she replied with just a suspicion of bitterness. 'And yet I was born in Jamaica.'

He rode away; once out of the ambit of her searching eyes his face fell to gravity. 'Poor girl,' he muttered. 'I am afraid she will feel stranger still before many weeks have passed.'

Chapter 16

DREGS OF BITTERNESS

'He come three times already, Mr. Joe, and he only know her for a week.'

'Well, Psyche, I suppose he likes her, and he's a young man, and lonely.'

'He has a girl, Mr. Joe, a brown girl, who me daughter don't know anything about, so he is not lonely. What he coming for?'

'I know all about his girl, Psyche, but she is not his companion. Don't you see he want somebody he can talk to as an equal, and be friendly with? He is a gentleman, and the baroness is a lady, and there is not very much people like them in Jamaica. No wonder Mr. O'Brian come here so often.'

'That's not all, Mr. Joe, an' you know it. If he didn't like her for herself he wouldn't come. She like him too: I see them together once last week, so I know. What does he mean, Mr. Joe?'

'I can't tell, Psyche,' answered Mr. Buxton in troubled tones, 'but if I guess me lady's character right, he will have to mean what *she* mean—not a doubt about that. She's more determined even than you was as a girl, Psyche, and when you was young you were a little hell.'

The comely black woman with the straight hair and aquiline nose smiled slightly. She knew that Mr. Buxton intended to pay her a compliment; also that he was sincere. Yes. She had been somewhat of a hell in her time to those who were her enemies, to those towards whom she felt antagonism. She could easily be the same now if sufficiently aroused. But her daughter was, if Mr. Buxton were to be believed, the fiercer, the more ruthless character of the two. She believed that, she felt proud of it. 'And yet,' she said aloud, 'her father was one of the sweetest, gentlest men that ever come to this country.'

'Yes, Psyche, but what about his father, or grandfather? You didn't know them; perhaps your daughter take after them. I've read or heard somewhere that the Huntingdons were terrible people in England. Your daughter may be like them.'

'Maybe; and if this man, Mr. O'Brian, try to treat her badly, I hope she will get even with him, Mr. Joe. I will try to help her. She's all I have in this world.'

Mr. Buxton answered nothing; he knew that that would be useless. And that afternoon, when Frederick O'Brian rode past his house towards the Great House, he followed the rider with troubled eyes.

Psyche came out gladly to meet her visitor; she welcomed him with outstretched arms. 'We are going for a ride, Fred,' she cried; 'let us go to Cowbend. I have sent to tell my old nurse that she may expect us.'

'Excellent. And now I could welcome a rum punch, though it ought, strictly speaking, to be drunk in the forenoon.'

'There seem to be no rules in Jamaica where drinking is concerned,' she laughed, 'and, my dear friend, you seem to have been drinking too much already today.'

'Nothing to speak of,' he protested; she looked quizzical but gave the order for the punch. She thought a little sadly: if only Frederick would drink a little less; if only he would get rid of this detestable Jamaica custom!

The rum punch was brought, consumed; it was strong and it stirred the brain of the man who drank it. He began to talk quickly, though he took care not to raise his voice.

'Psyche,' he said suddenly, 'do you know I have fallen in love with you?'

'I guessed as much after your second visit last week,

Fred,' she laughed. 'You are not very good at concealing your feelings, you know.'

'My God, you are a woman in a thousand! You see the fact and you admit it. Well, what are you going to do about it, my dear?'

'I? It is not I who am to do anything about it; surely it is you. Do you want to marry me, Fred?'

For some moments he stared at her dumbfounded. It was true, he knew, that white men were marrying coloured women in Jamaica these days; but they were hardly men of his position. Then he remembered that the women also were not of the baroness's position, that there were very few in the country indeed who, from any rational, reasonable social point of view, could be considered her equals. Yet it was not of marriage with her that he had been thinking. He forced himself to believe that he was not of the marrying type; that therefore he would not be insulting her if he suggested to her a free love relationship which was too common in this country to provoke any comment. He did not realise that in 1831 the Jamaica ethos, feeling, was rapidly though silently changing from what it had been, nor did he understand the baroness's character as well as old Buxton or her mother did. Why, if they loved one another, should they not live with one another? he had asked himself. Not openly, of course; he felt that to that she would have strong objections. But secretly, in so far as there could be secrecy in such affairs. She, however, now spoke distinctly about marriage. It was clear she did not realise she was but the bastard daughter of a former Jamaica proprietor, even if that proprietor had been an English nobleman, and that her mother, who had come as a slave girl from Africa, was still living. But at once, sitting there, his better nature won uppermost, and he remembered that all her adult life up to now had been spent in Europe, that she was the widow of a Frenchman who, most probably, would have in his heart of hearts regarded Frederick

O'Brian as so much dirt, and that she had a son who was actually the Baron de Brion. He tried to shift the subject. 'We must talk about this matter some other time, Psyche; I only wanted to bring it up casually today.'

This was no answer to her question, and she knew it. Her eyes were fixed on him as though they would pierce to the very core of his thoughts. The frown on her forehead, which had almost disappeared during the past few days, was distinctly visible now, the smouldering fire again burned in her eyes. But she would not press the subject: she had not introduced it; it must be brought up again by him. He would bring it up again—she knew that, and wondered what he would say on that occasion. He and the Buxtons were the only white people in the parish that she knew, and that alone was queer; but she realised now that she was not a white woman, though she could not intimately realise why that should in any way affect her. These people —well, they could hardly consider themselves her equals. Then why this nonsense, of which, it seemed, even Frederick was not entirely innocent? She put away these thoughts with a contemptuous, hardly perceptible gesture, and sprang to her feet. 'I think my horse is ready, Fred,' she said. 'Let us go riding now.'

They took the way to Cowbend and up to the cottage in which Psyche Huntingdon had lived for so many years, while keeping in touch with all that took place on Hope Vale and hearing every rumour and tale concerning the estate. Psyche greeted them with respect, asked if they would come in and have something to drink—rum punch, madeira, coffee? Lady de Brion refused for both; it was already growing dark, she said, they would not dismount. 'Then let me walk with you to the gate that lead to the nearest road to Hope Vale,' pleaded Psyche, and strode off as she spoke. The others followed on horseback; near to the gate that they approached they noticed a small group of people surrounding something stretched out upon the ground.

'A calf is sick there,' said O'Brian. 'What are you doing about it, Psyche?'

'It's been sick for some hours now, sir,' said Psyche, 'but it is in no pain. It will die tonight or tomorrow morning.'

'But surely you can save its life! Can't you drench it or something?'

'Nothing will save it now, sir; it eat something that has poisoned it; it must die.'

'If it vomited, my good woman . . .'

'When we found that it was sick it was too late to give it anything to make it vomit; nothing could touch the poison. But it does not suffer.'

The baroness glanced at the glazing eyes of the paralysed calf which did not even moan; involuntarily a chill seemed to envelop her and she shuddered. She glanced at the older woman's face; it was set, rigid, inscrutable. But in her eyes burned a sullen fire. To the baroness came the conviction that this scene of the motionless, dying calf had been purposely staged for Fred O'Brian and herself!

Then she asked herself why she thought this, and could find no credible answer. She smiled slightly, bade the elder woman goodbye, and, with her companion, rode away.

'Do you really believe in marriage, Psyche?'

'Yes.'

She and Frederick were sitting on the veranda of the Hope Vale Great House; it was almost a week after they had gone for the ride to Cowbend.

Dusk had fallen, though it was but six o'clock in the afternoon; and the short days and long nights of Jamaica had commenced. Fred had ridden over half an hour before; he said he was not certain that he would stay for dinner. 'It depends upon the answer I shall give him tonight,' thought his hostess; therefore she was not surprised at all at his question.

'But what is marriage? A mere formula, some words muttered over you by a parson, or a signature before a Government officer. It is nothing, really; whereas, if two people sincerely love one another——'

'They will not object to marrying, Fred, if they sincerely love one another. They will not mind the formula, or the signature, that binds them together forever: they will welcome it.'

'Well,' said he shortly, 'I am not a marrying man.'

'So you have said before, and you are not singular in this country. Hardly any men here seem to be marrying men; or, if they are married, they also observe a sort of system of polygamy. I am supposed to be a Jamaican myself, but I have lived so long out of this country, am so much a stranger here, that I confess everything seems new and very strange to me. . . .

'There is something else, too, which I might as well mention now. I have a son. He is the Baron de Brion. I am not prepared to give him a lot of Jamaican bastard brothers and sisters, Fred: in the first place, he would not acknowledge them; in the next place he would come, when old enough, to hate his mother, and he would be right. So, you see——'

'Psyche, Psyche, why do you assume that I am asking you to do all the things, or anything, that you consider impossible? What have I said to lead you to believe that?'

'You are not good at lying or at deception, Fred; you are naturally open and truthful. You know exactly what you have meant, and I have known it too. And I know the reason now. I was ignorant of it even two weeks ago, but enlightenment has come in the meantime, come in a flood. You feel you could not marry me and remain in Jamaica, and you also feel that if you left Plimsole you might lose it to some rascally Jamaica attorney, or that it would go to pieces. Either of which things would probably happen. You could leave Jamaica, of course, and we could live in

England; but it revolts you to think that you might be living on my money. I respect you for that, Fred, but it is not your only consideration. The money would be that of a—what do you call it?—mulattress I think is the term. Many men here would take that money gladly, would even rob the mulattress, but that you would not do, Fred. But in any case marriage with a mulattress revolts something within you, does it not? Fancy one of the great O'Brians— for I am certain that the O'Brians must be great, though I had never heard of them before I met you—allying himself with a Huntingdon, and with the widow of the late Baron de Brion, and with the mother of the present Baron de Brion. O, what a fall that would be!'

'Psyche!'

'Let me finish, Fred; what I am saying now has been accumulating in my heart for some days: it is better that I should get rid of it. I am much obliged that, as much as you could, you have sought to avoid insulting me in so many words. Yet you have acted in a way which any woman would have understood, and to me that has been an insult. We are not likely to meet again, Fred; our paths lie in different directions. Yet I believe that you love me, and I too love you, my dear, as you already know.'

'But, Psyche,' he pleaded, 'our Jamaica gentry . . .'

'I don't know what you are going to say, Fred, but I suspect that you are going to plead as an excuse for your conduct the prejudices of your Jamaica gentry. Isn't it a pity that among this gentry there are so few ladies and gentlemen? Hardly any, it seems. But you, after all, are not Jamaican, though you have been here many years, and you are naturally a gentleman, Fred. Therefore do not quote the Jamaica gentry. If you must mention any of them, try to think of the one or two you know who can honestly be regarded as gentlefolk. Yes, Daphne, what is it?'

Daphne, a maid as black as the ace of spades, had appeared at the door to enquire whether she should lay places at the dining-table for two. Her mistress answered promptly: 'For one only, Daphne; Mr. O'Brian is not staying for dinner.' Then she rose and looked expectantly at Fred O'Brian.

Daphne withdrew; Fred rose heavily to his feet. 'You are turning me out of your house, Psyche,' he muttered.

'That's perhaps best for both of us, Fred; at any rate, it gives you a sense of grievance that may be helpful to your self-respect. I know I am guilty of atrocious bad manners; but what can you expect from a mulattress?'

'Whoever called you that?' he stormed. 'Who put that idea into your head?'

'There are others of more or less my complexion on this estate; I have seen them. Then there has been the attitude of your gentry. And I have thought a little and put two and two together. Goodbye, Fred.'

He took her hand, clasped it warmly; in another minute she heard the hooves of his horse thundering away from the Great House. She buried her head on her arms on the table in front of her and wept as though her heart would break.

Then a rap sounded on the door that led into the sitting-room; she sat up sharply, wiped her eyes, and called out, 'Come in.' It was her old 'nurse', Psyche Huntingdon.

The elderly woman glanced keenly at the baroness, saw the tell-tale indications of tears in the face she gazed at, knew that Mr. O'Brian had left but a little while ago; she had, indeed, been at Hope Vale for some little time and had seen him come. She guessed far more of what had occurred than the baroness could possibly have imagined.

'Sit down, nurse,' said Lady de Brion.

Psyche Huntingdon sat on the edge of a mahogany-seated chair, solid and black and brilliant with polish; she handed a small package to the baroness.

'I brought these from Africa when I came here as a little girl, milady,' she said, 'and I gave them to your mother before she died. She asked me to give them to you some time; I should have sent them to England.'

'What are they, Psyche?'

'Poison beans. If you grind two of them up and give the powder to someone to drink, nothing can save that person from death, and no one will ever know what killed him, unless you talk about it.'

The younger woman started, stared, then opened the crinkled envelope curiously, and saw within it a few withered beans, six in all.

She laughed somewhat sadly: 'Three deaths are here, then?' and Psyche Huntingdon nodded solemnly.

'And you have had these for over thirty years, by your own account: has it never occurred to you that their potency is gone—I mean that they are useless now?' asked the baroness.

'You saw the calf the other evening, miss; it died that night: it had been given two of these beans by me: I wanted to know if they could still act. They can.'

'A deadly undiscoverable poison, eh?'

'Yes, ma'am.'

'Did my mother ever use these beans?' demanded the baroness suddenly, looking at Psyche Huntingdon with piercing eyes.

'Once I believe, ma'am, though she never talked much about it. A girl, a white girl, wanted to steal your father from her. Your mother killed that girl. She was right.'

'Well, I don't want to kill anyone, nurse; besides, I should say, if you are right about my mother, that she was entirely wrong; she was a murderess.'

'I am not sure, ma'am, that she really killed anyone,' the black woman hastened to say; 'I only speak what I have heard some other people say. But England is England and Jamaica Jamaica, and what may be wrong in England may be right in Jamaica.'

'This is the second time this evening that I have heard

that doctrine suggested,' smiled the baroness bitterly, 'and maybe both you and the other person who advanced it are right. I cannot accept it, though. Yet I will keep these beans, nurse; they seem to be the only memento I have of my mother. Where do you say she is buried?'

'In St. Andrew.'

'Some day before I leave Jamaica I hope to see her grave. Meantime I have much work to do. I will keep the beans carefully. God bless you, nurse.'

Psyche Huntingdon curtsied low. 'God bless you too, milady, an' keep you from all harm. Oh, God bless you.'

'Why are you crying, nurse?'

But the tall, sable woman with smouldering eyes and aquiline features was already disappearing through the door.

Chapter 17

PREPARATIONS

THE rumour was persisting, spreading; who had started it no one knew, but thousands of the slaves believed it; it gained credence with a rapidity that no new religious doctrine could have equalled even among a superstitious people.

The King of England had decreed that the slaves of Jamaica should become freemen at the end of the swiftly dying year, but the white masters were keeping the precious boon from the people and preparing to continue to hold them in bondage forever. That was the story now being told, and in a week it had overrun the borders of St. James and overflowed into the parishes of Trelawny and St. Ann and elsewhere. On the other hand the slave-owners, while loudly denying that Emancipation had yet come—and in this they spoke truth—also declaimed against it with terrible bitterness, thus proving that they knew its advent in the future to be sure and inevitable. In the presence of their household slaves, in their newspapers, they raved against the belief that the slaves would be freed and no penny of compensation given to the owners who would thus, in most instances, be irretrievably ruined. Always one heard of this proposed lack of compensation, and the mere thought of it fanned to fury the anger of the masters and mistresses throughout Jamaica. They screamed that they were about to be ruined. Everywhere they said bitterly that it was to this that English religion and philanthropy were bringing them at last.

It was two weeks after the baroness had sent away Frederick O'Brian, and since then nothing had passed

137

between them: not a note or a word. But in that fortnight the baroness had been busy; indeed she had set herself to work the very day after she had dismissed Frederick, and with an energy and resolution to which Jamaica was little accustomed.

In the morning, early, after her memorable last talk with Frederick O'Brian, she had sent for her former 'nurse'.

'You have heard these stories about the King making free all the slaves of Jamaica at the end of this year, haven't you, Psyche?'

'Yes, miss'—the Jamaica form of addressing even married women came very naturally to Psyche Huntingdon now—'Yes, miss, for some time, but a lot of people say they are not true.'

'They are quite true,' firmly asserted the baroness, 'but the owners do not want it to be believed. I am going to make arrangements with my lawyers here to free every man, woman and child who is a slave on Hope Vale at Christmas-time. You should do the same with your people on Cowbend, nurse.'

'But, milady, when we do that, we'll be poor compared to what we are now, an' then——'

'Nonsense! You have to feed and clothe the slaves in some sort of fashion, have you not? And you can no longer turn them off into the roads and streets to starve as in former days: that at least is against the law. Well, the slaves that are freed today will be seeking employment tomorrow, and the land you give them to cultivate for their sustenance, and the food and clothing you allow them, they will have to pay for. We at Hope Vale will pay our people wages after Christmas, and they will work for us. If you like I will compensate you for the slaves you set free on Cowbend.'

'Very well, miss, I will set them free; but I want no compensation. After all, everything I have is yours.'

'I have guessed that, nurse, for some time,' answered the baroness with a mirthless smile. 'But now there is something more for you to do, and I want you to preserve strict secrecy in regard to it. Not a word about it to Mr. Buxton even. Do you promise?'

'Yes, milady,' said the older woman, eyeing the baroness keenly and with a glint of fear in her eyes.

'Very well. These slaves in this and other parts of the island who expect to be free at the end of this year, they have leaders, have they not?'

'Yes, miss.'

'I want to get into touch with one or two of the most influential of those leaders: tonight if possible. You can tell them what you and I intend to do with our slaves—they would know in a very few days, anyhow, for I am seeing my Jamaica lawyers today. Can you bring one of them to see me here tonight?'

'It is possible, miss, but dangerous.'

'Never mind the danger; whom have you in mind?'

'There is a church-leader called Daddy Sharp; I can send him a message by Mashimba's son today: I hear he is at the Bay. If he get it, he will come tonight.'

'Ten o'clock will do. I am depending on you, nurse.'

'I will do whatever you want, miss; but remember you have powerful enemies round here an' they will be glad if you make a single mistake.'

The baroness laughed. 'Enemies? Why, I hardly know anyone in this parish. But assuming that my very existence is regarded as inimical, do I appear to be afraid of that?'

'You are afraid of nothing,' blurted out Psyche Huntingdon, 'and that is why I fear for you.'

'Don't,' smiled the baroness, but her smile was acid. 'I will see this man Sharp tonight, if he comes. Meantime, I am going to the Bay today to see my lawyers.'

'Can I come with you, milady?'

'Please. We shall begin a memorable thing within a few hours, nurse.'

The night was cool, for now it was early November. Sweet breezes wandered over the countryside; brilliant tropical stars shone down upon a scene which seemed to be one of perfect quiet and peace. Except for the occasional throbbing of drums here and there, a spacious silence enveloped the neighbourhood for miles and miles around; it was all serene and beautiful.

The Baroness de Brion stood just without the front door of the Hope Vale Great House looking about her and thinking. She knew that the throbbing of the drums but summoned some youths to a dance which, at this time of the year, when the slaves would be at work from early morning, was illegal and forbidden; but no one seemed to mind in these days this violation of ancient law and custom. The Negro village on Hope Vale, which might be seen from the Great House in daylight, was now concealed by darkness; not a light burned in any hut there though it was but about ten o'clock. 'Perfect peace,' she murmured—'on the surface. What lies beneath? Here they are contented enough, seem happy; but elsewhere? Calm, undisturbed, to the naked eye; hell in the heart and mind.'

She heard a sound, as of persons quietly approaching. She opened the door behind her and went into the dining-room, where a few candelabra burned. The domestic servants had been told from seven o'clock that evening that their services would not be required tonight. Some had wandered off to see their friends: they would not be back before midnight. Others had gone to bed. The house was empty save for the baroness herself.

In half a minute her old 'nurse' and a tall, black man entered the dining-room. Him she eyed scrutinisingly for a few moments, then seated herself. The other two stood and waited upon her words.

'You are Samuel Sharp?' she asked.

'Yes, ma'am.'

'You are a deacon or something in the Baptist Church?'

'Yes, ma'am.'

'And you have been telling the slaves about here that the King has granted them freedom, and that, on New Year's Day at latest, they will legally be free?'

He hesitated a while, then bravely replied:

'I hear so; I believe so; why shouldn't I say so?'

'But the Governor says the report isn't true,' broke in Psyche Huntingdon. 'So I hear.'

'Then the Governor is wrong,' interposed the baroness quietly, coolly, deliberately. 'He has to speak as he does because of the attitude of the slave-owners in Jamaica. Actually, legally, the slaves of Jamaica are already free. On Christmas Day and after no one can compel them to work.'

'Thank God,' breathed Samuel Sharp. 'God Almighty be praised!'

'Psyche herself found you in Montego Bay today, didn't she?' the baroness went on.

'Yes, ma'am, she told me she was going to send her headman's son, but that she come herself as she was in the Bay.'

'Good. We went to the Bay today in order to draw up manumission papers for all the slaves on Hope Vale, Cowbend, and the other properties that may be attached to them. This manumission will be effective from December 24th; meantime we have to make arrangements for hiring the slaves for wages after Christmas, and so on. Do you want to make that known at once, Sharp?'

'No, miss, no,' Psyche Huntingdon implored urgently. 'It will become known in plenty of time; but it will be better that Daddy Sharp shouldn't say a word about it; shouldn't let anybody know that he know.'

'Yes, ma'am; it is better I should say nothing until other people begin to talk.'

'I see. You both want to protect me. Against nothing!'

'Daddy Sharp promise me that he won't say a word of

what you tell him tonight about the King and the Jamaica
slaves, or anything else,' continued Psyche Huntingdon.
'We know you just come from England and must know the
truth, but we want to keep you' name out of it. Daddy
Sharp believe trouble is coming, an' you must not be
mixed up in it, me dar—milady.'

The baroness gazed steadily once more into the face of the
man who, standing there hale and hearty, vigorous and
determined, had not nevertheless three months of life left
to him, but within those coming months would end his
days upon a public gallows. The countenance was open,
frank: that of an honest man. But in the eyes there was a
gleam of fanaticism that could become a fiery flame; this
man was all in earnest and would die bravely when the
hour to yield up his life had struck. To the very last, in
spite of all persuasion, he would stoutly maintain that no
missionary in Jamaica had suggested to him that the slaves
would be free at the year's end or before, would stand
faithfully and truthfully by those in whom he believed;
and never, either, would he inculpate the baroness even by a
whisper, a suggestion, in the troubles that were approaching
and of which the ominous portents might be discerned on
every hand. The baroness shrugged her shoulders slightly.
'Every now and then,' she thought to herself, 'we do find
one who has not bowed the knee to Baal.'

She rose briskly. 'You and the others have much work
to do,' she said: 'you have to spread the glad tidings. Do
you want any money?'

He took five pounds from her as he had to move about;
she would gladly have given him fifty. Then he bowed
respectfully and, with Psyche Huntingdon, went away.

Left alone, the young woman placed her elbow on the
table by which she sat and plunged into meditation.
'That man knows who I am,' she thought; 'something in
his demeanour warned me of that. I think I too know now;
but I shall say nothing, and he and many others will say

nothing; he, indeed, looked proud that the daughter of Psyche Huntingdon should have become a baroness and the owner of Hope Vale. My "nurse"! Poor soul, she is torn between pride and fear. Not by a word would she hint that she is my mother, yet, after all, I was bound to learn that fact in time: somebody would have told me even had I not guessed it. Buxton must be well acquainted with all that is to be known concerning my Jamaica childhood, yet Buxton too is loyal. And Buxton is afraid of something.

'My uncle—so he was my father! I ought to have understood that long ago. How kind he was, how good. He never wanted me to come back to Jamaica; had he not died he would still have refused to let me come, and, because I loved him, I would have done what he wished. It would have broken his heart to know that his daughter was suffering as I am suffering now. Tonight I cannot be sorry he is dead.

'Poor Fred! He loves me, and I love him too, but how could he marry me here? Yet he could have gone with me to England and have lived there, my husband, for always. His pride about money is ridiculous. After all, he is still young and could find plenty to do in England or in Ireland. It is not in him to be merely a parasite. And at the worst he is not penniless.

'But he is weak. He doesn't know it, but he is weak—I am the stronger of the two. He cannot make up his mind as to what he should do: tonight he is either miserable, as I am, or drunk. He fears the local opinion of his kind and class, though he knows that I despise both it and them. And I? I shall go back to England and live there with the memory of him; but I have a son to care for, and that is much. In my old age I will encourage my boy to travel to this country and he will be worshipped here because he looks white and times will have changed, and because of his title and his wealth and his position. I shall smile at that when I am old.

'There will be a new Jamaica in twenty, thirty, or forty years' time, and I shall have helped to make it. By freeing my slaves next month, by telling Samuel Sharp without any reservation that the king has made the slaves in Jamaica free as from this year, I have struck a blow at Jamaica slavery from which it cannot recover. I have lighted a fire which rivers of blood will not be able to quench: there will be fire, there will be blood, but the flames will be triumphant. My mother thinks, fears, that I may be consumed in the flames I am lighting. What does that matter? But I believe she is wrong, for she and Sharp and Buxton, and all the older slaves on this property, would swear to lies if they thought that that would help me. Silly folk! As if, now, I cared anything about myself, or really had anything to fear.

'Slavery must end, and that swiftly: that is England's determination, and it is also mine. I know its curse now as I could never have guessed it before. During the rest of the time I shall spend in this country I will go about freely, attend every function I am entitled to attend, meet insolence with arrogance, stare down these middle-class people with eyes of contempt. I am fighting now. And we Huntingdons have always known how to fight.'

Chapter 18

AT THE BAZAAR

THE roads leading to Falmouth from the parish of St. James were thronged by the vehicles of the period which were on their way to the bazaar, or sale of work, in Falmouth, the chief town of Trelawny. Women rode in these carriages, some light, some heavy; the men went on horseback. The roads were wretched, miserable. In the colony there was no regular department for keeping these highways in order; subsidies were given to the members of the House of Assembly to enable them to maintain these public thoroughfares in some sort of repair; but the moneys thus granted were hardly ever accounted for satisfactorily, the work at best was never well done; so the roads were broken, unpaved, masses of dust when it was dry, watercourses and mud when it rained. But today there was to be a bazaar in the Falmouth Court House from about five o'clock in the afternoon; therefore early in the morning, with the November air still deliciously cool, the ladies and gentlemen of St. James and Trelawny began to take their way to Falmouth.

It was not the bazaar that was the attraction; it was the fact that the Colony's Governor and his wife, the Earl and Countess of Belmore, were just now making a brief tour of Jamaica's north-western parishes and would be at the function in Falmouth. Many of the island's gentry may have detested the Earl, yet they loved to bask in the sunshine of his presence; it also was good to show that a sale of work in benefit of the Established Church (which was by no means in a deplorable financial condition) would be handsomely patronised by the better classes who believed

in working for the Church so long as that institution did
nothing to interfere with their morals and mode of life.

From St. James came the baroness with the rest. The
distance she had to travel being not more than some twenty-
five miles, a change of horses half-way on the journey would
amply suffice for her convenient travel. It was early yet
when she arrived at Falmouth, a town she already knew.
Mr. Buxton had arranged that she should rest during the
warmer hours of the day at a semi-private lodging-house;
he had played upon her wealth, her title, successfully,
though the lodging-house-keeper, 'a brown female' as
almost all the lodging-house-keepers in Jamaica then were,
wondered what her white clientele would say to the
presence of this coloured lady if they all had to dine in
common.

But the baroness went straight to her room to lie down
and rest, and it was her English maid accompanying her
who ordered such refreshment to be sent up to their room
as both of them required; also, in addressing the 'brown
female' who kept the semi-lodging house in which Mr.
Buxton had secured a room for the baroness, Gladys spoke
as she might to a slave that could not understand courtesy:
issued commands instead of making requests. But the
method served. The female trembled and obeyed, realising
that Gladys was too formidable to be questioned respecting
the baroness. In Gladys's eyes there gleamed a challenge
which few would dare to take up.

In the intervening two weeks the Baroness de Brion had
seen nothing of Daddy Sharp, but, from Psyche, had heard
much about his movements. He and the other leaders of the
slaves had been extremely busy; while he, being a freeman,
could move about as he pleased. Already a rumour had
got about that at Christmas-time the slaves, unless set free
then by their masters, would rise. But the owners refused
to take these warnings seriously; not that they did not
believe that they were true but because it had always been

their habit, and that of their forefathers, to refrain from taking preventive action of any kind until a crisis was upon them. Activity meant exertion, and exertion implied a certain degree of discomfort. Perhaps everything would come right in the end, especially if one denounced loudly enough all the parties and principles to which one was opposed. Meantime, in unison with denunciation, one could always imbibe madeira and rum punch. Plenty of these. And one could talk sedition in the hope of frightening the British Government and Parliament thousands of miles away.

The Falmouth Court House was a stone structure built in the Georgian fashion; it was oblong in shape, it was of excellent proportions. On its first storey were the parish's court rooms and other public offices; on its second storey was the formal reception hall of the parish entered by two flights of steps leading upwards from the ground. It was in this hall that were to be found the largest and finest chandeliers in the colony, which, when the innumerable candles of them were lit, flashed in all the varied colours of the rainbow and made brilliant and sparkling the scene on which they shone. This was the pride of Trelawny; the boast was that there was nothing to equal it even in the capital of the country, St. Jago de la Vega. Its main entrance faced the sea, and when the great doors were thrown open the sea-breezes cooled the hall's interior, though the sun might be at its zenith outside.

Behind the Court House and to right and left of it was built the town. A great stone tank in the centre of a square provided the townsfolk with water; behind the tank was the open-air market of Falmouth where, on market days, the slaves and others brought their provisions, their cakes, their fruit, and, squatting on the ground with their edibles spread in front of them, sold their wares amidst an incessant chorus of chatter and laughter, the vendors as happy as the day was long. Sunday was the principal marketing day in the colony; and, whatever the hardships and grievances over which the slaves may have brooded on the secular days of the week, these seemed temporarily forgotten when men and women—women mainly—met in the market to chaffer and joke and scream with laughter: Sunday at least was theirs, and the miles between Falmouth market and their respective estates and cattle pens seemed as nothing in comparison with the enjoyment of the moment. But of late, at these Sunday markets, a note of seriousness was sounded again and again in these miscellaneous conversations. Again and again the word 'emancipation' was heard, and much of the talk was about the approaching freedom of the slaves.

The sides of the square behind the Falmouth Court House and reception hall were formed by shops and houses, each block divided by streets running outwards in different directions. If one wandered about the town one would see—which was not noticeable in other urban centres of the island—some houses with balconies built in front of the windows of the upper stories; for most of the larger houses in Falmouth were of two stories mainly. The lower floor might be a shop, store, or warehouse of some kind; the higher formed the residence of the family whose business was conducted below, or, possibly, in these days, was rented outright as a home. The open square, the balconied windows, strongly suggested Spanish influence, which was not strange with the island of Cuba so near. Time was when men from Cuba would be seen in Falmouth's streets and houses transacting business, legal and surreptitious, and when Spanish money was not only legal tender in Jamaica but almost the only gold and silver coin obtainable. This was still largely so in so far as the currency went. And Falmouth itself wore a slightly Spanish look.

The common people and members of the free mixed-blood population of ordinary status were assembled before five o'clock in the space around the Court House to greet the Governor, and to gaze upon the local grandees as these arrived for the bazaar. By five the town's chief hall was fairly thronged with members of the gentry, though it was known that the Governor would not be there before half past five at earliest, and might not remain for longer than an hour. Every minute after five o'clock witnessed the arrival of more people, and some of these represented the humbler orders of the neighbourhood's white population. Thus the Benedicts were present, Mrs. Benedict having dearly wanted to be at a bazaar which a Governor would attend. Happily the sun was already setting and the sea-breezes blew with a strength that whipped the sea's surface to commotion and filled the hall with saline coolness. This reduced the discomfort engendered by a crowd.

There ran a whisper through the hall. The word was passed quickly; the woman who owned Hope Vale, the woman whose mother was black and who was a bastard, had arrived. What effrontery! What impertinence! Surely things had come to a fine pass when, because full equality with the white people had been granted by law to the coloured people, this woman should have begun to take advantage of that and to appear amongst the gentlefolk today at a function which would be attended by the Governor and his lady themselves.

And she had begun to make trouble for the better classes already. They knew this, for surely the report that she was manumitting her slaves at Christmas must be correct, otherwise how could everyone be so certain of it? She was being held up as an example to other Jamaica slave-holders by some of the mischievous missionaries, renegade Englishmen and Scotsmen who ought never to have been allowed to enter the country; her name was on the tongue of every malcontent amongst the bondsmen, and these were growing more numerous every day. Well, if there should be trouble in Jamaica next month she would pay her due part of the penalty. A baroness! A mere French title. A Huntingdon!

Well, if every illegitimate brat was to begin to trace his
descent there would be plenty of royal blood even found
amongst the slaves of the West Indies. She had no business
to have slaves, and, if she did have them, it was morally
wrong for her to grant them freedom. She should stand with
her betters in the fight they were making against Emancipation, or for ample compensation at least should the
slaves be ultimately set free. Her betters?—but this woman
carried herself as though she had no betters in Jamaica, as
though she looked down upon her natural superiors, as
though she were someone and they were nothing. A
situation intolerable. Yet, they said frankly, they *were* her
betters, and so she should humbly follow their lead.
Meanwhile many of the male gentry of those estates who
had heard of her alluded to her (half-admiringly, it must
be admitted) as 'a froward bitch', but most of the women
spoke of her as a serpent, a curse, a being that should
not be spoken of—though constantly now they were speaking of her! Indeed they became particular instead of
general in their allusions. They boldly said she had been
Frederick O'Brian's mistress from the first day they had met,
until he had found out all about her intended wickedness,
her plot to stir up trouble amongst the slaves, and then had
deserted her as if she were a thing unclean. O'Brian, they
were whispering now, had done the right thing. He had
taught her a merited lesson.

The stalls for the sale of work were ranged along the two
sides of the reception hall; behind these stalls stood the
ladies, mostly young, who sold things at an exorbitant price
in aid of a Church which was not poor. At the rear end of
the room was a dais with space for half a dozen chairs.
Two chairs only were set upon it now for the Governor
and his wife. Two minutes after the Baroness de Brion
entered the Governor's party was announced.

His personal suite was small for those times; it consisted
of but four officers whose breasts were covered with tight-

fitting scarlet coats and silver medals. But there were other high functionaries also: these were half a dozen of the Jamaica Major-Generals, of whom it had been said that their name was legion. Each Major-General wore the sort of uniform he preferred, so at least there was diversity of dress amongst those in attendance upon His Excellency, even if these gentlemen were sadly lacking in military deportment. They were all members of the island's militia, but no one imagined that they had ever received a day's military training anywhere; yet, because they loved titles and uniforms, they and dozens like them had become Generals, always to the secret amusement of the professional soldier of whatever grade he might be.

The Governor's party at once began a tour of the room, Lady Belmore stopping every now and then to make some purchase. Beside the Governor walked the Custos of Trelawny, beside Lady Belmore was the Custos of St. Ann who was accompanying the Gubernatorial group in its tour through the north-western parishes but who had no official status whatever in Trelawny or at this function. This particular Custos, however, Mr. Richard Barrett, had heard of the Baroness de Brion, and, on seeing her now for the first time, easily guessed who she was. He thought that his colleague of Trelawny would make it a point to present her to the Governor and his wife; after all, she was in her way unique and was an estate owner as well. But the Custos of Trelawny marched by the baroness, and the Governor and the others followed perforce; as soon as they reached the dais again, however, Mr. Barrett whispered something to Lady Belmore, who in turn spoke a few words hastily to her husband. Then Lord Belmore did what was, for him, a characteristic thing.

He beckoned to two of his officers: one proceeded to where the baroness was standing, the other instantly sought, found, and placed a chair to the left of the Governor's. The young English officer, all scarlet and gold,

approached the baroness with a low bow; His Excellency
and Lady Belmore, he said, would be glad of her company
for a while. As he said this he offered his right arm. Placing
her fingers lightly upon it, the baroness was led up to the
dais through an avenue of wondering people. She made her
curtsy in the perfect court fashion of England, a fact that
Lady Belmore immediately recognised and appreciated.
His Excellency and his wife then shook hands with her.
His Excellency pointed to the vacant chair. 'Won't you
sit with us for a few moments, Lady de Brion?' he asked.
'I hear that you have but lately visited our island; my wife
intends, I know, to ask you to become our guest at King's
House, should you ever visit the capital.' All this he said
distinctly and so was overheard by many.

The Custos of St. Ann smiled; he took some credit to
himself (and rightly) for having brought this meeting about.
Others in that room were furious; but they said to themselves that this was exactly the sort of thing that you would
expect this Governor and his wife to do—they would ruin
the country before they left it. But there were also present
a few, a minority, who like Mr. Barrett approved of the
Governor's action. These were among the farseeing people
in Jamaica; they knew that a new situation was rapidly
coming to the birth, had indeed been born already, and
that those who believed that the habits and attitudes of
fifty years before might be maintained if sufficient insolence
and tenacity were shown were but little removed from
maniacs. As for the baroness, she took this courtesy from
the Governor and his lady with no change of facial expression whatever, though in her heart she greatly exulted
in it. She remained talking with Lady Belmore for a few
minutes, then glanced at the Governor to see whether he
chose that she should stay longer or go. He said pleasantly:

'Well, we shall surely be seeing you again, shortly,
Baroness,' which she correctly interpreted as an amiable
and friendly dismissal. Again she made her perfect curtsy

and went back to where Gladys, her maid, was standing.

Mr. and Mrs. Benedict were near at hand; they sought the eyes of the baroness and bowed; she smiled pleasantly as she replied. But there were others whose anger could in no wise be appeased. So when she asked the price of some hand-made dinner mats the lady before whose stall she stood snapped out: 'Those are sold.'

'What of these,' asked the baroness calmly, pointing to some others.

'They are five pounds a set.'

Almost immediately before an identical set had been disposed of at the same stall and by the same vendor for a guinea; the intention of this sudden exorbitant rise of price was therefore obvious. Gladys opened her lips to protest vigorously, but was silenced by a gesture from Lady de Brion. 'This bazaar is in aid of the Church, Gladys; therefore those who can pay ought to be made to do so. Will you take these mats, please?' She handed the amount charged to the stall-holder with a charming smile. Somehow the latter felt little.

The Governor's party left; the people began to overflow into the rooms below, where liquor could be had. The steps leading up to the reception hall were crowded, voices which had been subdued now became loud, sometimes arrogant and dictatorial. The baroness began to think it was time that she also should go; she had a journey of twenty-five miles before her that night. She lifted her eyes. Staring at her was Frederick O'Brian.

She shifted her gaze rapidly; even that brief glance had warned her that Fred had been drinking. Her whole being was flooded with bitterness; she wanted to avoid any public humiliation now, and Fred might be the cause of that. She knew him; courage of a sort he did not lack, and in the face of all that crowd he would have marched over to her, at the slightest sign of invitation on her part, and have called her loudly by her Christian name, thus proclaiming their friendship in the teeth of any opposition. And yet,

she reflected bitterly, he had shrunk from the thought of
an actual, legal marriage with her and had thus revealed to
her the depth and the strength of the intense prejudice which
still dominated the social life and conduct of Jamaica.

'Come,' she said abruptly to Gladys, and, protected by
the press of people between her and Frederick, made off
quickly in a direction opposite to that of his. He was still
staring at the spot where he had caught sight of her when
she passed behind him, reached the top of the entrance
stairs, and went down them quickly. She and Gladys
stepped towards the place where their carriage stood; it
had been arranged that they should leave the bazaar
directly for the journey to Hope Vale, hence they had had
a decent meal immediately before proceeding to the
bazaar. The vehicle's driver was Charles, Mashimba's son.
As soon as the baroness and her attendant were seated, he
started off at once in the direction of Hope Vale.

It was some minutes before it dawned upon Frederick
O'Brian that the baroness had eluded him and was no
longer at the bazaar. His face flushed with anger; he felt
he had been deliberately insulted. But Frederick, though he
had been drinking, was not drunk; he had not become
unreasonable—far from it. She had a right to avoid him
if she wished, he admitted to himself; after all, was it not
he who had offended her? He had not meant to do so, but
what else could he have done save what he did? What else;
yet he had not passed one happy hour since that last night
of his at Hope Vale; forever in his brain had recurred the
word, applied by himself to himself, 'coward, coward,
coward'. Always he seemed to hear it, and always it mad-
dened him; he was hearing it much louder now than ever
before. He hung his head; then remembered that men
were downstairs drinking. He would join them; he would
drink himself unconscious. Ignoring the salutations of
friends and acquaintances in the reception hall, he pushed
his way downstairs.

Chapter 19

THE MEETING

THE horses were in fine condition; in spite of wretched roads they arrived at Cowbend before midnight, after being changed only once midway on their journey.

The baroness was silent almost the whole length of the way, silent, morose and bitter.

Her frame of mind was dangerous, one might even say murderous, for she had been by no means ignorant of the sensation her appearance at the bazaar had created; she had guessed at some of the nasty, unkind, and even infamous things said about her, knew that the courtesy of the Governor and his wife had been resented—she believed by all. She now suspected that that courtesy had been specially emphasised because Lord Belmore wished to teach, through her, a lesson to people who might consider themselves her superior. She resented this; she must be accepted in her own right and not for any extraneous reason whatever; she silently fumed; she was disposed to be unjust even to the Governor and his lady. And at the back of her mind always was Frederick O'Brian and what she regarded as his contemptible action. That, more than anything else, was fuel to the fire of her hatred and her wrath.

Why could he not have followed her when she left the Falmouth reception room? He must have missed her almost immediately; if he had wished he could easily have trailed her; even had he found that she had left the town he could have overtaken her with ease; he was an excellent rider and his horses were among the best in St. James. But, no doubt, he was glad that she had disappeared, had been wishing that she would, and now was enjoying himself

with others of his kind—drinking, carousing, perhaps
mentioning her name with disparagement. Pouring contempt on her—No, Frederick would not do that, she in-
dignantly contradicted herself. At least he was a gentleman.
But he could have followed her had he been so minded.
Why had he refrained?

It is true that it was she who had sent him away from her
two weeks ago, but what man with red blood in his veins
would have minded that had he truly cared for the woman
he professed to love? How then could she shrink from the
conclusion that he had not wished to meet her that evening
in the Falmouth Court House? She was a mulattress, only
a woman fit to become the mistress of a white man—if he
were of O'Brian's class—not his legal companion and equal.
She, the widow of a de Brion! She, the daughter of a Huntingdon—for, yes, by God, her father had been Lord
Huntingdon and head and shoulders above all this rag-tag
and bob-tail of Jamaica, and he had loved her, educated
her, been proud of her, and had left her wealthy. She was as
much of a Huntingdon as though she had been born in
wedlock. And the Huntingdons, as she had long known
through her reading of the family records, suffered no
insult to pass unpunished, and brooked no slight at the
hands of anyone.

Unpunished. That was the dominant word in her mind
at this moment. An ineluctable determination that the
punishment should be widespread and terrible at once
emerged from her thinking.

'Charles,' she said quietly, 'drive to Cowbend; we shall
easily arrive there before midnight. I wish to speak to Miss
Psyche Huntingdon. You will take Miss Wilmot on to the
Hope Vale Great House afterwards.'

'I can wait for you at Cowbend, missis,' said Charles,
who did not at all approve of the baroness spending the
rest of the night at Cowbend, or going on to Hope Vale
with perhaps an indifferent escort.

'You are not to wait but to do precisely as I say,' she answered sharply; 'and you Gladys, don't wait up for me. I shall find my way to Hope Vale quite safely.'

'Yes, milady,' said her maid.

'But, your Baroness,' began Charles argumentatively, when he was acidly interrupted.

'Do you notice, Gladys,' said the baroness, 'how these people in Jamaica argue over everything? They evidently do not understand that an order is an order and must be obeyed.'

That silenced Charles, because, perhaps he recognised that it was perfectly true. He humped his shoulders and drove on sulkily.

They came to Cowbend; and, luckily, all the lights in the house were not yet extinguished. As the buggy drew up in front of the building's principal entrance, they heard movements inside. The baroness alighted quickly, then instructed Charles to drive on. He had no option but to obey.

Before the baroness could rap the front door opened and Psyche Huntingdon appeared. She was dressed as if for going out; she seemed surprised to see the baroness. The first words of the latter caused her eyes to open wide with astonishment and something like dread.

'I want, nurse,' said the baroness, 'to see some other leaders of the slaves besides Samuel Sharp. They must meet sometimes; I want to be at one of their meetings as soon as possible. Do you know where they gather, and when? Can you take me there?'

'When, miss?' enquired Psyche in a voice which seemed to her interlocutor to tremble.

'Any time. Tonight if possible. Are they meeting to-night?' she enquired shrewdly.

'They are, miss,' answered Psyche in a low voice. 'Daddy Sharp sent to tell me so only today. I am going there now.'

'Why were you going?'

'To hear what they intend to do, so as to tell you.'

'I will hear for myself. How did you propose to go?'

'I was going to ride, miss.'

'Very well, nurse; you can get me a horse and we'll go together. Is the place far?'

'About six miles, but half the way is uphill.'

'I see. A secret meeting in the hills: well, that precaution is sensible. Can you have a horse saddled at once?'

'I will saddle it myself, miss, but it is better I should go than you. Trouble is coming, an' you will run a risk. Better let me——'

'Please saddle the horse at once; I don't want to miss the men I should see, even if I hear but little of what they may have to say. They may have begun their meeting already.'

The tone in which this was said was decisive; Psyche had no option but to obey. But she sighed. She felt the clouds of trouble, of sorrow, of disaster closing upon her, on all sides pressing down. And she was powerless against them, for in the baroness she had met at last with a woman whose will was stronger than her own, perhaps because her own will was partly paralysed by an intense devotion to this daughter of hers who (she felt) must always be made to see in her a former nurse only and must never guess at the blood relationship that bound them irrevocably together.

A horse was soon saddled for the baroness; both women mounted and rode away. They went quietly for the first furlong or so, and then Psyche put her steed to the gallop, the other horse immediately accelerating its pace. After a while they came to rising ground on which large trees grew in great numbers. But the path here was wide enough for them to move abreast for some time; a mile further on they would be compelled to proceed in single file.

'Nurse,' the baroness said suddenly, her face hidden by the darkness but her voice distinct and vibrant, 'you told me the other day that you believed my mother had once used some of those poison beans you gave to me. She killed a woman with some of them, didn't she?'

Psyche gasped. Swiftly she cursed herself for having said so mad a thing when she had given the beans to the baroness. But she had even then pretended uncertainty. She must still do so, now and ever after.

'I told you what I heard, miss; not what I knew or believed. I think the story was a lie.'

In the darkness the face of the baroness grew grim. She knew she was now listening to lies and that never would she learn the truth from anyone, whatever she might believe. But of one thing she was certain: this woman riding by her side, her real mother, had been a murderess, had killed to prevent her man from being taken from her. But now she felt no horror at what Psyche Huntingdon had done: she could understand at last and, what was more, entirely sympathise. Psyche had but followed the good old law, the ancient plan, as a modern poet had expressed it. It was right in such a God-forsaken country as this that they should take, who had the power and they should keep who could: there was surely no other way. Her mother, evidently, had kept her father, even though someone who would have taken him from her suddenly died. Thus too the slave-owning plantocracy of Jamaica would do everything in their power to keep their slaves; it would be seen whether she, also a slave-owner, would not be able to wrest from them their possessions even at the price of ruin and destruction. In that struggle vast torrents of blood might flow.

The path narrowed; they must now ride in single file. Psyche pushed her horse forward, the baroness followed. Then, far and faint, the sound of chanting came at intervals to their ears. It was accompanied by the muffled throbbing of drums. They were gradually nearing the spot where the conspirators—for these persons who were meeting that night were conspirators—had gathered; and now Psyche Huntingdon began to move forward as quietly as might be, so that the sounds which their horses might make should attract as little attention as possible.

At walking pace they advanced to about a hundred yards of where a crowd was gathered, and because of the lights in the space before them, and of their elevation on horseback, they could see almost distinctly while they themselves remained in obscurity.

An oblong space among the trees had been cleared some time before; about the four sides of it stood or crouched a number of men and women gazing at women who, clothed in white and red, now whirled in a sort of frenzied dance and uttered words that were interpreted as 'prophecies' by a few men who, draped all in scarlet, and with pointed caps of the same colour on their heads, repeated aloud what the inspired speakers said. Foam issued from the mouths of the dancers, occasionally they screamed as if in madness, again and again one or more of them would fall writhing to the ground, her limbs twitching, her eyes staring. Only a few of those present were clothed in white and red; the audience, the men and women who waited anxiously for the oracle to speak, were garbed in the everyday dress of the slaves, in which they had stolen forth to attend this meeting. They were people from different neighbouring estates; their clothing was rank with dirt and sweat; the odour that came from their unwashed bodies was almost overpowering. A grotesque, almost repulsive lot of human beings they seemed, until one remembered that many of them were prepared to fight for their freedom at the risk of their lives: then indeed one gazed upon them with somewhat different eyes.

The baroness stared at the scene before her with a look of horror: whatever she might have expected it certainly was not this. Psyche looked on with indifference, even while she uttered a far-carrying whistle that brought two of the scarlet-clad interpreters striding in her direction. Evidently they had expected her; this indeed was not the first occasion on which she had been a witness of these gatherings, which reminded her much of reunions she had attended as a girl in distant Africa. Others of that crowd, which must have numbered at least three hundred souls, heard the whistle also, saw two of their leaders move swiftly in its direction. But evidently they had become accustomed to these summonses, for they continued with their chanting and their dancing undisturbed.

'It's Daddy Sharp and Colonel Johnston, miss,' whispered Psyche to the baroness as the men approached.

Samuel Sharp went straight to the baroness; could his face have been seen, it would have been observed to wear a look of shame.

'I'm sorry for all this, ma'am,' he said at once, indicating the open space radiant from the light of flaming torches, the dancing, writhing women, the watchful men interpreting the words that fell from foaming lips; 'as a deacon of the Baptist Church I should have nothing to do with it. But what can I do? These people are savages.'

The baroness smiled at this naïve apology; she understood the Christian deacon to be making excuses for practices which were distinctly African and pagan. And a prelude to rebellion and murder.

The other man joined Sharp: 'This is Colonel Johnston, ma'am,' said Daddy Sharp.

'And how did you get your military title, Colonel?' the baroness asked.

'The Lord gave it to me, your Baroness'—so he already knows who I am, she thought—'The Lord giveth, and the Lord taketh away: blessed be the name of the Lord.'

'Remember that, when the day of trial comes, Colonel,' said the baroness softly; 'for that day is coming soon.'

'I know it, ma'am, an' we is all prepare. The voice of God is crying out to us an' we mus' heed it at last. I am prepared to die so that my people may go free.'

'And those other men that I see in that clearing?'

'They are also prepared, every one of them. Captain Dove and Captain Wellington are prepared. There is others, your baroness-ship, but I only speak of those who are here tonight. They are slaves, but God has put fire into their hearts. And they know they will have to fight for freedom.'

'Let them and those they lead never forget that: unless they fight they are lost. Shall I speak to these people, Colonel Johnston.'

'Yes, milady, yes,' he answered eagerly, but simultaneously there broke from Psyche Huntingdon and Samuel Sharp the cry—

'No, milady, no!'

'And why not?'

It was Psyche who instantly thought out an answer to this question—

'They are ignorant people, miss, not like Colonel Johnston here. And they will believe, from what you say, that they must strike at once even if you tell them not to. There will be confusion and failure; and you know they are not ready yet.'

'That is true enough, I suppose,' commented the baroness thoughtfully; 'even my slaves on Hope Vale have not yet been freed, and these people are anxious now to do something—anything. Listen, Colonel Johnston: tell all these people, and others, and let them in their turn tell yet others, that after the Christmas holidays not one of them should return to work as slaves. If any effort is made to coerce them, they must desert the estates and pens and strike for their liberty. They must fight—do you understand? *fight!* There is no alternative. They will only be striving to take what the King of England has already granted to them. For already they are free.'

Her voice was low, and shaking with passion. The men who heard her remembered that she was the mistress of Hope Vale and the daughter of a great English lord. They bowed low to her as to their supreme leader.

'You will need money for the work you have to do,' she went on decisively. 'Here is some. Tomorrow I will send each of you twenty pounds more, and sixty pounds extra for the other leaders of your movement. My nurse will see that you get it. Good night.'

She backed her horse, then turned its head in the opposite direction when the trees and the ground permitted. Psyche Huntingdon followed.

The older woman tried to find some consolation in the fact that her daughter had only talked to Sharp and Johnston and that none of the others at that meeting could possibly swear it was she who had been there that night. Yet Psyche knew that Johnston would spread far and wide the news that the baroness had been there, had urged rebellion, had given them money to pay what expenses they might incur. The hawks were hovering low; soon they would sweep to their quarry's destruction. But to this, although she must know it, the Baroness de Brion seemed utterly indifferent.

'Ride with me to Hope Vale,' was all she said on the journey homeward.

There was no moon; but the stars were brilliant. They went in darkness, but Psyche knew the way. She marvelled at the strength, both physical and mental, shown by the baroness; she had driven to and from Falmouth during the last twenty-four hours, and yet she had gone to a rebel gathering on her return from Falmouth and still was acting and planning with icy determination. What did it mean? What was the cause of these peculiar actions?

Only when they had reached the Hope Vale Great House, and Psyche had positively declined to sleep there for the rest of the night—indeed, it was already morning—the baroness said:

'I know you do not approve of what I am doing, nurse, but I know what I do. The slave-owners of this country are determined to fight to keep the people in bondage, I am as

resolved that the people shall go free. If a sacrifice is necessary, I am content to supply it in my own person: my
fathers in far-away England have done as much again and
again. My actions are deliberate. And, remember, the
people of England are absolutely determined that slavery
shall be abolished in this country.'

'Yes, miss, but if we wait a little, nobody will suffer.
Why not leave everything to the English people?'

'That would not do. By acting for England, as well as
for the slaves, I act for myself also, do you understand that?'

'Yes,' breathed Psyche Huntingdon almost inaudibly.

'And only I can act for myself,' she continued passionately; her long-suppressed feelings finding vent in an
hysterical outburst at last. 'And I shall not feel satisfied
until I see the Great Houses and the sugar houses of this
and other parishes going up in flames. All of them, do you
hear? All of them!'

'I hear; I understand,' whispered Psyche Huntingdon.
She turned to ride away, with the dawn paling the over-
arching skies. 'God have mercy!' she muttered to herself.

Chapter 20

MR. MORTON'S VIEW

WHEN Frederick got to the lower storey of the Court House he found there a fairly large number of people. The court rooms were on either side of the building; the centre of the building therefore formed a long corridor wide enough for people to move about in freely. Against the walls on either hand tables had been placed and these were heaped with bottles containing liquor, bowls of sugar, and of limes—there was, of course, no ice—and dozens of tumblers. The drink was not much varied: madeira and rum punch. But one might easily get drunk upon these were one inclined to inebriation.

Frederick walked towards one of the tables, angry with Jamaica, angry with himself, angry with the baroness, uncertain what to do. He had missed the baroness, it hadn't dawned upon him that she had immediately left the town or was hoping and longing that he would follow her. He imagined that she was still mad with him for having insulted her two weeks ago, although, he fiercely assured himself, he had really intended no insult. He supposed now that she would never forgive him. Fred did not know very much about the mental and emotional processes of women in love.

There were eight or ten men round the table up to which he walked; they were buying themselves and one another drinks—in the interest of true religion, as they would have said. They fell suddenly silent as he appeared amongst them, a circumstance which convinced him at once that he had been the subject of their conversation. Which was true; but they had not been speaking ill of him. On the contrary, those who had not been silent had been vocal in his praise. These believed that he had put 'that woman' in her place some time ago; and of that they strongly approved.

Therefore the talk again broke out almost immediately after he had taken his stand in the little crowd and had ordered a drink. Among the talkers was Mr. Arthur Benedict, who, except at race meetings and functions for the aid and succour of the Church, like this one, would never be found in the circle of his social superiors. This gentleman had not accompanied his brother and sister-in-law upstairs. But he had just heard all about the especially courteous treatment which the baroness had received from the Earl and Countess of Belmore, and he bitterly resented it on general principles. It was he who now took up the thread of the interrupted conversation.

'Let me congratulate you, sir,' he said to O'Brian. 'You know how these upstart people are to be treated, how we should conduct ourselves towards these mulattos. You have treated that woman, who calls herself a baroness or something of the sort, in just the fashion we all ought to treat her. I want to congratulate you, sir.'

'And who may you be?' asked Frederick in an ominously quiet tone.

Arthur Benedict was surprised, startled. Even drunkenness he felt should not cause him to be even temporarily forgotten by a man who had met him several times in Montego Bay and who must very well know who he was. It seemed, indeed, as though Mr. O'Brian wanted to insult him!

In the group amongst whom they were standing was an elderly man of sixty-five; he had had almost nothing to drink and had been listening with a quizzical smile to what the others had been saying in disparagement of the people of mixed blood. He noticed Frederick's tone, noticed especially the way in which Fred was looking at

Arthur Benedict. That the latter had blundered he knew. That O'Brian was disposed to make a quarrel of this blunder was apparent to him if to no one else at that moment.

Benedict did not know how to answer that cutting question 'And who may you be?' While he struggled to find words the older man, Mr. Morton by name, dipped quietly into the talk.

'We all of us, I suspect, have coloured children, or have had. Isn't it nonsense, then, to speak of these insultingly, even if behind their backs? They have equal rights with all of us now, and we silently resented it when they hadn't—where our own offspring were concerned of course. And I can tell you, gentlemen, that the day will come when we'll regret all this wild talk, in this country, about colour.'

'Oh, everybody knows you have half a dozen mulatto bastards,' sneered Benedict.

'Quite so; two of them are waiting for me outside now,' admitted the old man suavely. 'They are nearly white, by the way, and I am not sure that they could not long ago have claimed the privileges granted to those of a certain complexion here, and who were termed "white by law". Such persons were made white by a law passed some time ago; and a good few of us now are "white by law", Benedict. Do you understand what I mean?'

Arthur Benedict turned pale with fear and anger. He knew that Mr. Morton's allusion was to himself and to his brother; he had heard it said that their father had been 'white by law,' while there was no doubt whatever that Morton himself was purely white by blood. For Morton was an Englishman who had now been in the island for over forty years, had brought up an illegitimate family whom he would leave well off, and who was noted for politeness of manner coupled with a scathing form of speech. He was a gentleman by birth as well as by breeding; that was recognised by all with whom he came into contact.

No one knew anything about his English past, about which he never spoke, but all knew that his children were devoted to him and that his sons would not have hesitated to kill at the old man's behest (or even without it) had any man grievously insulted their father.

'Look here, Morton,' began Arthur Benedict, too mad with rage now to think much about consequences, when he was interrupted by Fred.

'I believe, Mr. Benedict,' observed Frederick elaborately, 'I believe that you were speaking to me just a moment or two ago. I asked who you might be, and you have not answered. But I remember now: you are a hanger-on, are you not, upon your unfortunate brother, Mr. Rupert Benedict? I understand that the Baroness de Brion bought your brother's property the other day and that in another couple of weeks you will be going with him to the east end of this island. You seem to follow him everywhere; but how he must wish that he could shake you off! A parasite, you know, is never a pleasant thing, whether it be a louse or a human being. You seem to be a mixture of both, and——'

'Steady now!' cried Mr. Morton. 'Remember, O'Brian, that if this man challenges you to a duel you cannot accept the challenge. You cannot fight with one who is so obviously your inferior.'

'You damned low-down Englishman,' gasped Arthur.

'I was expecting you to say something of the sort,' replied Mr. Morton coolly. 'Now I am the insulted one, not Mr. O'Brian, who, really, has insulted you. You will therefore oblige me by leaving this room at once, Mr. Benedict—at once, do you hear? Or shall I call in one of my sons to expel you? In fact, I think I will do that myself.' And without a moment's pause Mr. Morton, who in spite of his years was abnormally strong and active, caught hold of Arthur and began with surprising ease to propel him towards one of the Court House's open doors.

In a minute or so the incident was ended; Mr. Arthur

Benedict had been flung outside with an ease and dexterity which brought a smile even to the lips of those who secretly sympathised with his futile ferocity. But he was not exactly of their class, and they did not imagine that he would endeavour to get even with either Morton or O'Brian. So they dismissed him almost immediately from their minds.

Mr. Morton having returned, observed that Frederick was eyeing man after man in that company in the hope (it seemed) that someone would say something unpleasant that would be an excuse for a fight, perhaps even for bloodshed. Fred's eyes, too, occasionally strayed to the men at the other tables who had witnessed the brief affair between Mr. Morton and Arthur Benedict but had not interfered. Fred, he saw, was spoiling for a row. 'The damned fool,' he muttered, but slipped his arm under that of O'Brian, with the words:

'Give me a minute of your time, Fred.'

Silently Frederick O'Brian allowed himself to be led out of the Court House, into the open, towards the seashore where crested waves were now shining silver-white in the starlight. A breeze from the sea cooled his brow; almost immediately he felt that he was sober.

'Yes,' said Morton, as though in answer to a question, though Frederick had asked none: 'Yes, they were talking about you and the Baroness de Brion, but I could easily see that they had got hold of the wrong story. Care to tell me the truth of it, Fred?'

'Why should I?' demanded Frederick harshly.

'No obligation in the world to do so, my dear fellow; if you like, treat my curiosity but as an old man's damned inquisitiveness.'

'I notice, Mr. Morton, that you do not threaten me with your sons' vengeance, or with your own,' answered O'Brian with a short laugh.

'No. Bless my soul, why should I?'

'Because you are a gentleman and my very good and

true friend,' cried Frederick, suddenly feeling ashamed of himself, 'while I am a half-drunken bore. No—don't deny that: I know that I have been speaking to you rudely. But I am glad you ask me what had happened between the baroness—Psyche—and myself. I wish I could have told it to someone long ago.'

Under a sky now sparkling with stars, with the façade of the Court House so near to them, Frederick told his tale. He was himself surprised to find how little there was to tell as he and Mr. Morton paced up and down the stretch of sandy shore towards which they had unconsciously strolled.

'You see, Morton, how impossible it would be for me to marry her and remain in this country?' concluded O'Brian. 'We should have no friends of our own class except, perhaps, a few men. I know I should grow soured and discontented, and maybe become a drunkard—if, indeed,' he added bitterly, 'I am not one already.'

'You are not a drunkard,' said Mr. Morton firmly, 'but, also, Fred—if you will allow me to say so—you are not showing the strength and decision of character I should have expected from you. What keeps you from marrying this girl, selling your property here, and beginning life again in England? She, too, isn't poor. I understand she is rich.'

'I will not live on her money.'

'Who said that you should?'

'What could I turn to in England at my age?'

'Your age?' cried Morton, genuinely surprised; then he laughed loudly. 'Why, my boy, you are not yet forty. You seem little more than a boy to me.'

'But what could I do in England?' persisted Frederick.

'I cannot say specifically; but even in these days Plimsole could fetch you many thousands of pounds if you sold at once. You haven't any mortgage on it, I suppose?'

'No, it is unencumbered.'

'Well, given a man of your education and general

ability, and with some capital, and with a wife that is rich, I should say that you would have no difficulty in falling on your feet in England at once. She'll be somebody over there, you know, even if she does not appear to count for much over here.'

'What precisely do you mean by that, Mr. Morton?'

'This: that she *does* count for a great deal over here, in spite of our general pretence. And we are all beginning to realise it.'

Fred looked puzzled; Mr. Morton smiled and continued.

'She has arranged that all her slaves shall be freed at Christmas. Who is going to follow that example? Yet slaves on other properties in this country will not be content to see one lot of them set free all at once while they continue in bondage, especially as they have got hold of the idea that the King has made them free but that their owners are withholding from them the boon of freedom. Your baroness, my dear Frederick, has lighted a fire in this island that will not easily be put out, and I believe that she has done so purposely. She has foreseen clearly the consequences of her act. I don't say she is not human: her father decidedly was. But in her lone fight against the Jamaica slave-holders she is actuated by bitter hatred. I can understand that.'

'Are you too against her?'

'Would I be talking to you in this way if I were? No; I think emancipation certain, but I want to get some compensation for my slaves, and I believe there will be compensation from the British Government. The Baroness de Brion can do without it; I cannot. I have my family to think of.'

'Yes, you have a fairly large family,' murmured Frederick abstractedly. Then he changed the subject abruptly. 'Do you think they can do anything to her if they imagine she has encouraged this belief about the King having made the Jamaican slaves free?'

'They can try,' answered the other dryly, 'and they will

certainly try. Your baroness is going shortly to need all the friends she can get, unless I am mistaken.'

'She can count on me,' asseverated Frederick warmly, 'and I believe that she can count upon you also.'

'I shall try to be just, Fred, but remember that in the last resort I have to stand by my own people in this country, even if I dislike most of them; and there is not one of my children who would think I was acting wisely if I agreed to emancipation without compensation.'

'Which is to say that the only big-hearted and courageous person in this country is Psyche,' cried O'Brian. 'But I always thought so.'

'A lover's belief,' smiled Mr. Morton; 'yet I have no doubt that you are right. But even while you think the world of the baroness, Fred, you will not marry her. I know it would be foolish of you to do so and stay in Jamaica; in fact, you couldn't. I could; but you are different.'

'You could . . . ?'

'Yes. You see, I am going to marry the mother of my children—soon. What does it matter what old Morton does? *She* has never suggested that I marry her, nor have my sons. They don't care sixpence. But my two daughters—they are my youngest children, you know. I have simply got to do what they want.'

'Funny world,' laughed Fred.

'Very funny. But you also find it very grim, my boy. You are in love with this woman; yet, because you fear the opinion of some people here, you will not marry her. And because she is coloured you won't even go to England to marry her there, but talk about not wishing to live upon her money. Why don't you try to be honest with yourself, Fred?'

'I am honest with myself, and you have no right to mis-interpret my reasons and attitude,' rejoined the younger man sharply.

'When you come to think over what I have said, you

will see that I have not misinterpreted your reasons, Fred. You will find that it is you, yourself, who have sought to hide those reasons from yourself. You have not the same amount of prejudice—colour prejudice—that some white folk have in Jamaica, but there is much of it in you still, and it is strong enough to keep you from doing what your affections and your respect for the character of the baroness would impel you to do. It may keep you so always. I shall say no more upon this subject to you: after all, I have no right to do so. But you gave me the opportunity of speaking, tonight, and I have taken advantage of it.

'I shall be married before the end of this year, Fred, but the wedding will be very quiet, and hardly anybody will believe it has really taken place. I shall not ask you to come.'

'I shall be glad to come,' asserted Frederick warmly.

'And I shall be glad that you do not, and so will not invite you,' laughed Mr. Morton. 'Will you return to Plimsole now?'

'I suppose so.'

'Then we shall ride part of the way together. For some miles our direction is the same.'

Chapter 21

MR. MORTON INTERVENES

THERE was tension in the air. Everyone felt it, though few would admit it. The slaves went about their work sullenly for the most part, but with an expression of expectation on their faces; their masters were holding meetings here and there in the north-western parishes, passing resolutions, defying both the British and the Jamaica Governments, and talking openly, before their house servants, of their intention to pay no attention whatever to anything the Imperial authorities might command.

Naturally, what they said was transmitted to the field workers, and more often than not extraordinarily exaggerated. The Christmas holidays were approaching, too, the time when, as was customary, the slaves would be given three days' vacation in which to make revelry and enjoy themselves. At such a time, usually, their mistresses would help to deck the Christmas 'sets' out with finery; these 'sets' were rival bands of dancers representing the Reds and the Blues; each 'set' went about garbed mainly in red or in blue, dancing, singing, scorning one another, and the white and coloured slaveholders took the part of their respective people and spared nothing in order that their Reds or Blues might be more flashingly attired than the rest.

No one knew the origin of these 'sets': some believed that the Blues represented the sailors or Navy, the Reds the soldiers or Army, between whom there had always been some rivalry in Jamaica. Others spoke of the custom as African, but of this there was no proof whatever. So far as one might judge, the idea of the 'sets' may have been introduced in earlier times by some educated slave-owner who knew of the rival chariot races of Ancient Rome, where Reds and Blues strove for popularity and mastery and whole cities were fiercely divided into Red and Blue factions.

These 'sets' had become a permanent part of the Christmas festivities in Jamaica, but today there was an apparent reluctance of the slaves to become Red or Blue dancers, and an equal indisposition of the owners to help them make the holidays a thing of uproarious merriment. Each party was, in fact, eyeing the other with bitter, resentful, suspicious eyes. The Baroness de Brion heard this, smiled acidly, and said something about the slow but sure grinding of the mills of God.

Word went round that as Christmas would this year fall on a Sunday, Sunday would be counted as one of the three to which the slaves now considered themselves entitled. But Sunday had for some time been regarded as an ordinary holiday; therefore it was murmured that the slaves ought to be given Monday, Tuesday and Wednesday this Christmastide, Sunday not being counted.

It was the baroness who first had suggested this to Daddy Sharp. As soon as she heard of the intention of the slave-owners or their overseers to count Sunday as one of the three holidays, she had sent for the deacon. He came obediently, at about ten o'clock at night.

'You should spread the word, Deacon,' said the baroness, 'that the slaves ought not to regard Sunday as one of their three days' holiday; they should not go back to work on the 28th, as they will be ordered to do. You understand?'

'Yes, your Baroness. They won't go to work till Thursday 29th, and even then——'

'Just so. Their freedom ought to be proclaimed with the holidays. It should begin with the 1st of January; indeed earlier. I should tell the people that, if I were you.'

'I will, ma'am.'

'Excellent. When do you have another "meeting"?'

'Tomorrow night, ma'am.'

'Tell your co-workers what I have said. If many of the slaves submit to this new proposed imposition, that will indicate that they are ready to submit to anything else, and for ever.'

The Baroness sat still and silent for some time after Deacon Sharp had left. She was half-reclining in a large easy chair made of mahogany with leather back and seating. A large cushion pillowed her head. She was thinking deeply; in two weeks at the most her work would be completed, or, rather, its results would have begun to be seen by all. Soon it would be known that her own people would be free on Christmas Eve; they themselves knew this already. The effect in this parish would be tremendous. It was not to be believed that the bondsmen would willingly return to work anywhere after that; and decidedly they would not regard Sunday, the next Christmas Day, as one of their special holidays. Not after Samuel Sharp had transmitted to them her words and advice.

There was nothing now to do but to wait and think. But waiting meant tension, and thinking was a horror.

It was about eleven o'clock; it was time she went to bed.

She strolled to the front door; opened it and went out upon the steps. The earth was silvered by the moon, the green of cane and of the trees stood out greyish in the moonlight, the mountains on the horizon looked ghostly; she fancied she heard the sound of distant drumming. She listened intently. Yes; the drums were sounding; she suspected that there must now be gatherings about the countryside every night. They were a prelude to what was about to happen, a rehearsal of that orgy of fire and blood that she had deliberately determined should take place in Jamaica.

Was that the sound of a horse's hooves? Faintly it came to her, then more loudly; it was certain that someone was riding through the property. It might be Mr. Buxton's son, or he himself. Well, it did not concern her.

She stood there looking out upon the scene, calm outwardly, a volcano beneath the surface. Since that afternoon in Falmouth she had not seen Fred, had heard no word about him. He was lost to her forever. Only revenge could be hers in the days and weeks to come.

The sound of hooves grew louder. The horse that she had heard was coming towards the Great House.

She saw it; it was being ridden by a white man, an elderly man whom she could not recall even having seen before. He reined in when he came in front of her. 'A chance in a hundred, and I took it,' he cried out. 'I feared, Baroness, that you might long since have been asleep, but I knew there was a possibility that you might still be awake. One should act on possibilities.'

He swung himself off the horse as he spoke, and ran up the few steps leading to the veranda of the Great House. She noticed that as he did so he swept off his hat. His manner was that of a gentleman and an equal.

'Allow me to introduce myself, Baroness,' he said: 'My name is Morton. Christopher Morton. I have had the pleasure of seeing you before, but I don't think you have remarked me anywhere. After all,' he laughed gaily, 'I am not remarkable.'

'Perhaps you are,' she said dryly, and held out her hand. 'A visit to a stranger and a lady near midnight is not a customary thing even in this country, I should imagine.'

'Anything is customary in this country,' he asseverated. 'We have no rules. I have lived here forty years now, and——'

'From what part of England did you come?' she enquired, interrupting him.

He told her casually.

'And you say your name is Christopher Morton?' she mused. 'Surely you must be connected with the Mortons that were neighbours of the Huntingdons long before I was born. My father was here; yet he never spoke of you to me in England. Why?'

'Your father left Jamaica before I came to this part of the island,' he replied quietly, 'so we never met. And, really, it doesn't matter who I was before I became a West Indian colonist, does it? I came to this country expecting to drink myself to death. I got a job, I worked hard, actually in time made money—I was practically a pauper in England, you know.'

'Your father's fault.'

'Perhaps. It doesn't matter now. Well, I got in with a coloured woman of some means but very poorly educated. She had ability, though; I owe her a great deal. She is still alive; we are married. My wedding took place only the other day.'

'Won't you come inside, Sir Christopher?'

'Mr. Morton, please remember. Now and always. You will remember, won't you?'

'If you prefer that.'

She led the way into the veranda where they would sit. Only one candle burned dimly in a sconce. On that and on the moonlight they must depend for illumination.

She seated herself in the chair her father had always preferred. He selected a mahogany chair with polished wooden seat and sloping back. 'You are wondering what has brought me here tonight?' he asked.

'Yes.'

'Frederick. Frederick O'Brian.'

'Did he send you, Mr. Morton?'

'No. He doesn't know I am here, doesn't even know that I have ever seen you.'

'Then I cannot understand why you have come.'

'I have come to ask you to send for him.'

The baroness sat bolt upright in her chair. 'Why should I send for him?' she demanded sharply. 'If he wishes to see

me surely he knows where to find me. I do not understand
you, Mr. Morton.'

'And yet the matter is simple,' said Morton quietly.
'You see, I had a conversation with Frederick the evening
of the Falmouth Bazaar. I had prevented a quarrel between
him and a man called Arthur Benedict, a person of no
consequence whatever. But the quarrel was about you;
Benedict wished to say impertinent things about you and
Fred was going to beat him within an inch of his life when
I interfered. Then——'

'How precisely did you interfere?'

'Oh, I said something to Benedict that he did not like
and he answered me impertinently. So I put him out of the
building at once. It was all over in a couple of minutes.'

'Surely you might have allowed Frederick to punish this
man, Arthur Benedict, Mr. Morton. Did you think he
would have cared about the consequences?' she asked
abruptly.

'How like a woman! You mean, Baroness, that you would
have preferred Fred to fight what you are inclined to think
were your battles and that I deprived him of the opportunity of playing the hero by intervening. But I did not
want your name to be mixed up in any sordid row; besides,
Fred might very easily have killed the scallawag, and you
would not have liked that. Try to see this matter clearly,
dear lady. The planters of many parishes are already saying
that you are largely responsible for the slaves' attitude, that
you are deliberately stirring up trouble amongst them, that
if there is any outbreak it can easily be traced to you.
Do you want a sordid fight over you or your name in ad-
dition to the burden you already have to carry?'

'Do you believe what the planters say of me?' she demanded, ignoring his question.

'Why, yes, I do,' he replied. 'It is quite true, isn't it?
How far you have yet gone I do not know, of course, but I
guess it is pretty far. I don't think Fred guesses half of what

you have done: I know, for instance, that you have seen the slave leader they call Daddy Sharp, but Fred does not know that. Sharp is a fanatic who will strike shortly; that is certain. You will be accused of complicity; but even the boldest of your accusers may hesitate as to what he says of you when it is known that you are either the wife of Frederick O'Brian or engaged to be married to him, and that you both are going back to England.'

'That will not be known, Mr. Morton.' She rose suddenly and spoke to her visitor standing. 'Frederick might have become engaged to me, instead of that he offered me his "protection", wanted me to become his leman. Me, a Huntingdon! Surely he was mad when he spoke! But the truth is that he had become infected with your prejudices here and could not bring himself to offer me honourable marriage.

'I know now the truth as I never had guessed at it before. I was born here. I have Negro blood in my veins. That has condemned me in the eyes of your aristocracy—such as it is. But I should not say "your aristocracy", Sir Christopher, for you can correctly estimate them quite as well as I, and you do not belong to their order at all. I must apologise.'

'Not at all,' he said quietly. 'I have just told you that I am married to a Jamaica coloured woman.'

'For the sake of your children, is it not? Well, they or their children will become the dominant people in this country in time and may look down upon those who are visibly dark, for that seems to be the way of this place. As to what they may be saying about me, it is quite true that I have helped the people of this neighbourhood to understand that they are human beings with rights, and that England thinks that of them. And I do know Samuel Sharp and have told him what he should tell the slaves. Sharp was here but half an hour before you came, Mr. Morton. And, understand me well, I shall rejoice if my words assist to set on fire every sugar estate and cattle property in St. James and Hanover and Trelawny—in the entire island in fact. That is what I am hoping. And what I say to you now is by no means private or between ourselves alone. You may broadcast it to the four corners of the earth!'

She ceased, panting. Her voice had vibrated as she had continued to speak; he could not see her features, but he guessed that they were working as though affected by a spasm: he knew that at last she had spoken out of the depths of her soul. Her tortured spirit had found some vent at last. He felt that, if the worse came to the worst, she herself would lead great bodies of rebellious slaves.

'Won't you sit down?' he said, and when she resumed her seat—

'So you do not give a thought to Frederick?' he questioned, thus bringing her down from exalted emotional heights to what, after all, was really nearer to her than the freedom of every slave in Jamaica.

'Does he give a thought to me?' she demanded bitterly.

'Yes. He is always thinking of you. I was at his house this evening, immediately before I came to see you. He was drinking. He is always drinking now. He will become a drunkard or a murderer if he does not stop. You can stop him by sending for him.'

'He is not so weak as you suggest,' she cried, impelled to defend Frederick as a man of strong character against what might be said of him even by someone who loved him well.

'I do not say that he is weak at all, Baroness,' answered Mr. Morton diplomatically; 'but it is true that he is drinking far too much. He believes he has offended you beyond the possibility of forgiveness: hence his despair. Have you never thought of that?'

'But how could I send for him?' she cried, and her tone was different now from that in which she had railed but a few minutes before; it was gentle, plaintive, as of one who wished to be convinced. 'And what should I say to him if he came? Have you thought of that?'

'Yes. You need not say anything definite to him about marriage; leave that to him. But you can tell him you have forgiven him his blunders of the past and see no reason why you two should not be friends. Within a day or two, perhaps within a few minutes, you will have him asking you to marry him. He wants to do that, you see, but has a foolish idea in his head that you can never or will never forgive him. So instead of coming to see you he drinks.'

Silence fell between the baroness and Mr. Morton for a minute or two, then the baroness spoke.

'If Fred wants me he will come to me, Mr. Morton; I am a woman and my instinct tells me that. I should only be making myself cheap by sending for him.'

'There speaks vanity and pride,' said Morton bitterly. 'Both of you are proud. You may ruin one another.'

'It is for Fred to make the first advance,' said the baroness stubbornly. 'Why haven't you spoken to him?'

'You are a rich woman,' he replied evasively; 'you must remember that Fred naturally shrinks from it being thought that he was marrying you for your money.'

'Those who wished to think so would think so anyhow, Mr. Morton. And we are both in Jamaica now, and I would not have Fred or anyone else imagine that I, whom you would call a coloured woman, was running after him because he was a white man.'

'Very well, Baroness; but you can surely have no objection to my saying to Fred that you have already fully forgiven him for any foolish thing he may have said to you sometime ago?'

'No-o,' she said slowly; then, more quickly and firmly, 'No!'

'Then I shall say goodbye now; it must be nearly one o'clock. Not at all a proper hour for a man to be leaving a lady's house!'

'Oh, it is quite proper here if the woman is coloured, isn't it?'

'Why so bitter, my child?' laughed Mr. Morton, as though he were speaking to one of his own daughters. 'You—you who are so different——'

'Not so different from any other woman in Jamaica; don't imagine that. I speak for many women tonight.'

'Well, go to bed now, and try to sleep. And remember never to call me Sir Christopher again; I have never used a title that in any case dies with me. I never imagined the secret would be so easily guessed. My own children will never know of it.'

'Is that due to pride or vanity on your part?' she questioned with a ghost of a smile.

'To common sense merely,' he laughed. 'I am afraid that my children, if they knew about the title, would begin to give themselves unnecessary and ridiculous airs. They are only human, you know.'

'And so am I,' replied the baroness; 'please never forget that.'

Chapter 22

FRED'S DECISION

'PSYCHE!'

She whirled round swiftly, delighted, and from her lips broke the cry of her heart, 'Fred!'

She had been standing in the huge, sombre dining-room of the Great House, her elbows resting on the shining surface of the silver-laden mahogany sideboard. Her hands formed a cup in which her face rested; with her back to the main door of the dining-room she had been plunged in thought. She had felt deserted, utterly alone; the shouts of the people on the estate as they made ready for their merrymaking of Christmas Eve conveyed no meaning to her ears, seemed hardly to reach them indeed. She was alone; now she must tread the path she had marked out for herself without a kindly voice to whisper words of comfort or support. She had sown the wind; she must reap the whirlwind, whatever it might be.

Her own slaves were free; others in that parish and in neighbouring parishes would be demanding their freedom fiercely in a day or two. And if refusal came, as come it would, the smouldering embers of hate and wrath would burst into flame and at least half the island would be like a volcano suddenly erupting. She would be charged with having created all the hell that was to come; she felt crushed beneath this burden, yet not for a moment would she now throw it from her. She must bear it to the end. But it was bitter, bitter that she alone must do this, unhelped, unfriended, with only black looks and bitter hate about her. Then suddenly came the cry from the well-known beloved voice—'Psyche!' It was Fred at last.

Swiftly, impulsively, she moved towards him: 'Darling, I did not expect you,' she stammered between laughter and tears.

'I should have come before,' he cried loudly, seizing her outstretched hands. 'Morton told me so again and again within the last two weeks. But I was proud, or stupid—I think it was stupidity that kept me away, Psyche.

'I lied to myself. I said I was poor and you were rich, though in my heart I knew I was not so poor. I have made money in the past and have not spent all of it; besides I am strong and I can work. But I chose to deceive myself; I would not honestly face the truth. It was Morton who made me do it, told me that if I wanted you I must come to you— that you would never send for me. And here I am at last!'

'Come to the veranda,' she said, still bubbling over with joy. 'We will sit there and talk as in old times. Old times? It is only a few weeks ago since you were here, Fred; but things seem to have moved quickly since then, and what happened a month ago appears as though it happened long, long since.'

On the dim veranda, lighted as it was by a single candle, he looked down into her face and saw eyes which struggled to keep back the tears of delight that strove to overflow. Without another word he took her in his arms and kissed her tenderly, she making not the slightest struggle but rather acting as though she had reached her goal at last.

'Psyche,' he said, and his voice was that of a man who had made up his mind and would brook no contradiction, 'Psyche, I told my lawyer today that Plimsole is to be sold. But perhaps before it is, you and I will leave this parish for Kingston, will be married in Kingston, and then will sail from Jamaica for ever—it was fated to be so, darling, from the beginning, and I am glad that I have seen the truth.'

'When do you think we can go, Fred?' she asked.

He was seated now in one of the big leather armchairs

of the Great House, and she was on his knees, no longer the
dominant, self-willed, resolute mistress of Hope Vale, not
at all like the proud widow of Baron de Brion or a descend-
ant of a Huntingdon, but rather like an eager girl willing
to be led, to let others do the choosing for her, to obey the
man whom she loved above everything else on earth. He
answered at once.

'Tonight is Saturday. Sunday, Monday and Tuesday we
shall be able to do nothing. Not before Wednesday shall we
be able to send someone to Kingston to make arrangements
for our wedding by special licence, for our lodgings, and
also for our passages to England. So next week we shall still
be here, dear, but in the first week of the New Year we
should have left St. James for ever. It is a pity we have
remained so long.'

She grew sober as a thought seemed suddenly to strike
her. It was something that had not crossed her mind before.

'You know, of course, Fred,' she muttered, 'that on
Wednesday at latest will be decided whether the slaves on
the various properties here shall go back to their work or
not. Through some of their leaders, I have advised them not
to. And under any circumstances they would refuse to
regard tomorrow as one of the special holidays to which
they are entitled; they look upon Sunday as already theirs
by right.'

She paused for a moment, then resumed: 'Their owners
have decided differently. It seems, indeed, that the slave-
holders are determined to force the issue, have decided that
the slaves shall consider themselves more powerless than
they really are or than the Government intends that they
shall be. So on Wednesday there may begin a reign of
terror in St. James, in Trelawny, in Hanover and elsewhere, and I am going to be held responsible for it. I shall
be here to face my responsibility. I am glad that even if I
would I could not escape it during the coming week.'

'I shall face it with you,' answered Frederick O'Brian

with a laugh that sounded like a roar. 'What you have done is right for me, and I will maintain that right everywhere in Jamaica. Give those who are your enemies not a thought, darling. They fight you and me together, and by God I think that we two shall be hard to beat!'

'But you still have slaves, Fred.'

'I shan't after tomorrow. All the bondspeople of Plimsole will be told within twenty-four hours that they are free; Plimsole will be sold with only free men living on it. Then we shall conscientiously stand together, Psyche.'

'You are so good,' she murmured, 'so very good. You are giving up so much because of me.' He felt her head pressed closely against his chest. She was weeping.

'There is no goodness in acting as I am acting, darling,' he retorted gently. 'I have thought over all that you have done, and I am satisfied that you are right. I have thought over all that I have done, and I have felt ashamed of it. Now at length, I repeat, we stand together. You can hardly guess how happy that makes me.'

'I think,' she answered, 'that this is the happiest hour of my life; I do not believe that at any other time we shall quite reach the peak on which we stand at this moment, Fred: the past all forgotten, the present great with achievement, the future shining with hope.'

Through the gloom of the night came the distant sounds of merriment the newly freed people were making in the Negro village of Hope Vale. Through the darkness shot faint gleams of fires that were burning outside the many huts on the plantation. Friendly fires these were, cooking for the feast of tomorrow as well as for the jollification of tonight, when no adult would sleep. Perhaps this too was the happiest moment in the lives of people who but that morning had been slaves.

'Let us go out to the village,' said the baroness suddenly. 'Let us witness for ourselves the rejoicings of these people. Tomorrow yours at Plimsole will also give themselves over to joy, but after that, Fred, there may be terrible happenings in St. James.'

'How shall we go?' he asked, ignoring her direful prophecy. She was dwelling too much upon the sadness and the sorrow that might come, he thought.

'We can ride.' She stretched out her hand, seized a heavy velvet cord and pulled it sharply. Somewhere to the rear of the house a bell clanged; presently a servant came hurrying in. If he was surprised to see the baroness sitting on the knees of Mr. Frederick O'Brian he displayed no astonishment in his attitude or in his tone of voice as he said, 'yes, missis?'

'My horse: saddle him quickly and bring him round to the front. Mr. O'Brian and I are riding to the village.'

The servant bowed and hurried away; very shortly afterwards he led a saddled horse to the foot of the front steps. Then the baroness, who in the meantime had hurried to her room, put on a bonnet, and thrown a scarf round her shoulders, ran down the steps with Fred O'Brian, where both mounted the waiting horses.

They rode towards the village; nearing it, their advent was greeted by the clamorous barking of dogs, without at least one of which no Negro family considered itself properly equipped. Here the fires, seen but as small specks of flame from the Great House, lighted up the village from end to end through its entire depth, and on each one of them some pot was boiling or pan frying, while from the communal oven of the village came the odour of roasting pig. Most of the children were still awake and were leaping about joyously, although many of them knew nothing about freedom. Men and women too were laughing and shouting; their cries would have seemed foolish to those who did not know the inner cause and reason of their uncontrollable merriment, their giggles, their constant movement, their intense excitement.

They heard the vociferous barking of the dogs, saw the

baroness and Mr. O'Brian emerge from the shadows into the light; instantly they began to gather in a crowd before them, to bow to them and to curtsy, and to call out blessings upon the baroness's head. She laughed and waved her whip in salutation, while Fred thrust his hand into his trousers pocket, pulled out a handful of loose change and flung it laughingly amongst the crowd. At this there was a wild scramble for the showering coin, a determined struggle on the part of everyone to become the possessor of even a single coin. Nevertheless, amidst all this scrambling and shouting perfect good humour prevailed. There was too much contentment in the hearts of the people gathered in Hope Vale's village tonight for anger to manifest itself for a moment.

The smoke from the flaming wood fires curled upwards, losing itself in the air above; in the distance the great hills could be sensed if not distinctly seen. Coconut trees thrust their slender stems towards the sky, below the village the cane fields rustled in the cool night air. In other parts of Hope Vale lights also shone as the white men employed on the property under Mr. Buxton busied themselves with preparations for the Christmas holidays, and perhaps wondered what would come when these were over.

'Buxton, of course, knows of what you have done, Psyche: does he approve?' asked Frederick.

'Yes; when he saw that I was determined. But I doubt that even now my old nurse, Psyche Huntingdon, approves. She is a slave-owner by nature, Fred; besides, she thinks that I am drawing a storm upon my head.'

'Upon our heads be it,' he answered in high spirits, as they both retraced their way to the Great House. 'My headman will make my proclamation of freedom on Plimsole shortly after daybreak, though I think that some of the slaves there already guess at what is coming. I have ordered my overseer to give the people an ox to be roasted in celebration of their new status.'

'And Buxton has also given my people an ox,' laughed the baroness. 'It will be roasted tomorrow. Our thoughts and wishes seem to have been running on parallel lines, Fred.'

'On identical lines,' he answered, and when they came to the Great House they left their horses standing by the front steps and strolled up and down slowly, making plans for the future as they thought, but in reality indulging in a lover's dream in which there was more exclamation than coherent talk. What stood out conspicuously in their minds and hearts was the knowledge, the sweet blessed feeling, that the doubts, the fears, the hesitations of the past were scattered at last; that in a few weeks' time they would leave this country for good as man and wife, after having perhaps forced upon its people the swift solution of a problem that had somehow to be solved—the problem of freedom, of the emancipation of human beings like themselves.

As he kissed her for the last time that night, before springing into his saddle, he said suddenly—'Won't you ride over to Plimsole early in the morning, Psyche, and see my people given their freedom?'

'Why, yes,' she cried quickly; 'what time shall I come?'

'Say seven o'clock, and then I will tell my overseer and other employees that we are to be married shortly; after that, and after we have drunk a Christmas punch at Plimsole, we might ride back to this place and have our "second breakfast" together. Will not that be ideal?'

'Good, Fred; it shall be as you say,' she laughed; then with shining eyes she watched him ride away until he was lost in the night's cool darkness.

Chapter 23

CHRISTMAS DAY

THE day had passed in a glory of sunshine, in loud revelry, in merriment that seemed at times triumphant, then defiant. Night had now come again, a soft dark night illumined with innumerable stars. But still the beating of drums, the rhythmic clapping of hands, the dancing, the singing continued much as it had done throughout the day. Yet here and there, especially among the more thoughtful bondspeople of the parish, some anxious faces showed. These awaited the aftermath of Christmas with saddened hearts.

Psyche Huntingdon stood that night outside her wooden house at Cowbend talking to the ancient Mashimba, and her brow was furrowed with care.

Mashimba had come to see her that evening, to wish her luck and prosperity. He had been greeted by a woman oppressed with a vague sorrow, the result of an endless foreboding.

'You hear the news, Mashimba?' she enquired, and strangely enough she slipped back into the language of her childhood, the African dialect which she hardly spoke in these days even to the old man who had come with her from distant Africa so many years ago.

He understood her, although the words were pronounced by a tongue that had almost forgotten them. He answered in English.

'No, Miss Psyche, what is it?'

'Mr. O'Brian say he is going to marry my dau—the baroness, and the news is going round and round the parish. Then the slaves on Hope Vale are free from today, and Mr.

191

O'Brian has made his people on Plimsole free. An' I hear
that the slaves on the other properties round here will not
go back to work when the holidays are over on Tuesday
night. So there is going to be fighting.'

'Don't the baroness know this, Miss Psyche, an' Mr.
O'Brian, too?'

'I think so,' murmured the woman wearily; 'she must
know it. An' Mr. O'Brian must know it too, even more than
she. But they won't take heed, Mashimba; I saw them ride
into Hope Vale today; they looked like two mad people.
They are at the Great House now, and I don't think they
are giving one thought to what is going to happen in this
parish this week.'

She fell to silence, and after a while the old man crept
away to think over what had been said to him. He was old
now and tired; it seemed to him tonight that it mattered
nothing any longer what anybody did: after all, they all
would soon be dead. Psyche remained standing at the
threshold of her front door hour after hour when he had
gone, staring in the direction of the Great House, although
she could not see it. Again and again she asked herself,
'What will happen?' but the secrets of the future she could
not read.

Yet she was wrong in thinking that the baroness and
Frederick O'Brian at the Great House were treating the
future with scorn. They knew only too well how grimly
serious it was. . . .

In the dining-room of the Hope Vale Great House the
baroness and Frederick O'Brian sat at dinner, and the room
blazed with a profusion of light which caused to flash and
sparkle the crystal and silver spread out on the great
mahogany dining-table and the huge sideboard. Four
servants assisted the two. For them it was a great day.
As she had promised, the baroness had early ridden over to
Plimsole and, standing beside her lover on the platform

on which terminated the broad flight of stone steps leading to the upper entrance of Plimsole's Great House, had heard the headman of O'Brian's estate announce the manumission of every slave on Plimsole. Then Frederick had turned to the few white men in his employment.

'Gentlemen,' he said to them quietly, 'I shall be leaving Plimsole shortly; it is for sale; it will doubtless be purchased by someone who will retain you in his employment. Meantime I have arranged with my lawyers that you shall continue employed on the property until it passes out of my hands. I am going to England with the Baroness de Brion; we shall be married in Kingston before we go. Gentlemen, I wish you a very merry Christmas.'

During his little speech the baroness stood erect, the upper part of her slim figure displayed to advantage by the fashionable English riding habit she had worn that morning. Her golden-coloured skin, her eyes set wide apart, dark, and sparkling now with pride and with delight, her firm chin and long upper lip, gave a note of distinction to her countenance. The white men assembled saw her suddenly from a point of view quite different from that with which they had casually glanced at her when she had ridden or driven by Plimsole on different occasions. They lifted their hats and bowed to her, the oldest of them venturing to murmur the congratulations of all—he was a tough and shrewd Scotsman. All of them thought she looked extremely handsome, and with an inner astonishment they began to realise that her demeanour was by no means timid and diffident, but gracious, as though she wished to be kind to them all! She made a movement towards the group that stood clustered on the broad platform to the left of herself and Frederick. Her hand went out in a friendly gesture: 'Thank you, gentlemen,' she smiled, and by that smile she won their sincere allegiance.

After that she and Frederick O'Brian drank an 'egg punch' made by one of the ancient domestics of Plimsole,

G

an old woman famed for her skill in making drinks. Then they had ridden over to Hope Vale for 'second breakfast': it was after this meal that Frederick had proposed a drive somewhere.

'And perhaps, my lady, you will invite me to Christmas dinner,' he added. 'You never seem to have thought of that.'

'No, darling, I have not; I have only thought of my happiness since last night.'

'Well,' said he, 'I am a human being with an extra-ordinary appetite, and if you are able to do without much food, I am not.'

'Stay until dinner, then,' she suggested. 'When we come back from our drive to the Bay you can rest in one of the rooms, and then we will celebrate Christmas as perhaps it has never been celebrated before in the Hope Vale Great House.'

Then a thought seemed to strike her. 'Could we not call on the Mortons?' she suggested.

'We could,' said Frederick; 'midday calls are not infrequent in Jamaica, especially if one stays to lunch.'

'Have you ever been there, Fred?'

'No; I have met Morton elsewhere, principally in Montego Bay. I suspect, Psyche, that his daughters are now a bit of a problem to him. You see, yielding to the solicitations of his wife, he had them educated in England; and we all know here that mamma has a touch of colour, and that sons and daughters alike are illegitimate. All that effectually bars them from such society as we have in this parish. I have heard that the girls were wild about this and that one of their first moves to repair the situation was to insist upon papa and mamma getting married. But I don't know that that will have any effect.'

Fred laughed. 'Papa and mamma lived quite happily unmarried, and mamma's practical abilities, besides money she inherited from her father, made Morton's fortune.

How they are going to get on together now that they are
man and wife I really cannot guess; but I suppose that after
living nearly forty years together marriage will make no
difference to them.'

'We will go to see them now,' said the baroness decisively.
'The Morton girls were right, Fred; it was high time that
their father ceased to live with their mother and became her
lawful husband. He ought to have done it at the beginning.'

'Well,' said Fred smiling, 'the lady didn't ask for it, and
I doubt if forty years ago Morton would have got on as well
as he has done had it been known that his wife was a
coloured woman, though as his mistress she was all right.
So, after all, everything seems to have turned out for the
best.'

Wolmer's Castle, as Mr. Morton's property in St. James
was called, was not very far from Hope Vale. Rapid driving
in a comparatively light trap drawn by a pair of fresh strong
horses brought the couple there in about an hour. The
baroness was accustomed to the appearance of Jamaica
plantations by this and could note with approval the neatness of the fields of canes, the various buildings of the
estate—the cooper, the carpenter, the blacksmith shops—
the great trees that shaded these, the interspersed groves
of fruit trees, the babbling river that turned the sugar mill.
And she loved the bright blue skies that everywhere hung
over this tropical world, and the gay laughter of the slaves,
though she knew that only too often that disguised or
concealed the cruel crack of the driver's whip.

Up a well-laid-out driveway the carriage proceeded until
it reached the wood and stone building which had been
incongruously called "a castle" by one of its former
proprietors, a large one-storied residence, the single storey
being built some seven feet above the ground's surface and
approached by the inevitable flight of marble-topped steps.

A servant ran down the steps to meet them; another
appeared from somewhere in the rear of the building to

hold their horses. 'Is Mrs. Morton in?' the baroness enquired.

The slave stared at her for a second, noticed her complexion, then looked at Mr. Frederick O'Brian. He obviously was a white man; who was this woman? the domestic asked in his mind. If she was the gentleman's 'housekeeper' she would not be at all welcome to the Misses Morton—they would not receive or associate with any gentleman's mistress. And they were young ladies to be feared. However, the house slave could do nothing about it. To the astonishment of Frederick, though not to that of the baroness, the man answered: 'Lady and Sir Christopher Morton are in.'

'Then please tell them that Mr. Frederick O'Brian and the Baroness de Brion have called to see them,' answered the baroness with that touch of hauteur which she could so well show when dealing with servants who were inclined to be insolent.

The man was impressed by her tone; bowed and asked if they would enter the house while he informed Lady Morton of their arrival.

Both nodded, and in a minute they were seated in a cool, darkened drawing-room furnished with the heavy, highly polished Jamaica mahogany furniture of the period, the three long sofas having hard horsehair cushions on their seats.

Inside the house Frederick whispered to Psyche:

'What on earth is the meaning of this? I know that Morton married Miss Julie, as she used to be called, only the other day. But I do not see that that makes her Lady Morton any more than it makes him Sir Christopher Morton!'

'Yet he *is* Sir Christopher, Fred,' answered the baroness quietly. 'You see, he comes from my part of my county in England, and we knew his family formerly. I believed I was the only person aware that he was the last legitimate scion of his race living; but it is clear that his newly married wife has found it out. Poor Sir Christopher! I am wondering now if it will be as pleasant to live with Lady Morton as with Miss Julie, as I think you called her.'

At that moment a brisk step was heard, and Morton, striding energetically as was his wont, made his appearance.

'I don't think you will see my wife today,' he said, as he shook hands heartily, 'but my daughters will be here presently. And I guess, baroness, you have discovered that what we imagined to be a secret between you and me only is now known to all my family!'

He laughed heartily.

'As a matter of fact,' he continued, 'I found out only at the beginning of last week that not only did my wife know that I was Sir Christopher Morton but that she had known it for some time. She seemed to have been going over my papers years ago—which she had a right to do—and so made the discovery. She promptly informed my daughters and sons of the useless title after we were married, and though my sons take the fact indifferently, my daughters regard it very seriously indeed. They say they are going to marry Englishmen or Scotsmen: on that they are determined.'

'And they will, too, Morton; they can do so in Jamaica if they like,' O'Brian pointed out.

'But not to men of the class in which they have been brought up, Frederick,' the father reminded him. 'They will have some money, and, although I say it myself, they are smart, well educated, handsome girls. And only twenty and eighteen. No; I have arranged to send them back to England: if they care to come out to Jamaica in the future, that is their business. But they will marry in England; as a matter of fact I think that Gloria, my elder girl, has a beau in London now. They have been here but a little while, and they say they are sick and tired of Jamaica. There is no proper place for them here, I fear, though there may be one before I die. Their mother wants them to go away, too, and I myself think it is better so, even though I know that the Jamaica of ten years hence will be very different from the Jamaica of today.'

Even while he spoke a peremptory voice was heard drawling out orders to the house domestics. And such a drawl! It was typical of most of the ladies and better situated women of Jamaica, but it sounded like a foreign tongue to the baroness and even to Frederick O'Brian. 'That must be mamma,' thought the baroness with slightly uplifted brows; but just then one of the side doors opened and in came the Misses Morton, in whose demeanour a consciousness of grace and beauty was subtly mingled with defiance because of the disabilities under which they had discovered during the last six months that they suffered in Jamaica.

But Frederick O'Brian sprang to his feet, all gallantry and deference, for he saw at once that the girls were ladies and he wished to assure them of his personal esteem. He saw too that even in Jamaica they could easily be taken for white women of a very superior class by those who did not know of them. His sincerity was unmistakable.

They sat and talked for a little, the baroness refusing an invitation to lunch by saying that they had already arranged to have lunch—a late lunch—at Hope Vale—and that she dared not disappoint her servants.

Was it true, asked the elder of the girls, that she had manumitted all her slaves?

'Yes, it is true,' said the baroness; 'yesterday'; at which answer they both looked doubtful.

'We cannot afford to do that,' said Gloria after a short pause. 'Papa believes that there will be compensation when Emancipation comes, and we must wait for the compensation. The slaves on our property are really better off than many English villagers and farm hands that I know. So why should they make trouble before they are legally set free? Besides, the Government can always deal with trouble,' Gloria added with assurance.

'I don't think those estates which treat their Negroes properly have anything to fear,' said the baroness calmly as she rose to go; 'but those that have neglected the clear warnings and indications of the time—well, they must take their chances, and I am sure your father will agree with this.'

'I do,' said Mr. Morton—who still refused to answer to 'Sir Christopher' although his wife now insisted that she should be addressed as Lady Morton on every possible occasion, while his daughters thoroughly approved of this.

'Speaking of trouble, Frederick, don't you think we might ride over this parish and speak to the people before the holidays are over? We might do some good; in any case we cannot possibly do any harm.'

'I agree,' said Frederick heartily, and thus on the spur of the moment an arrangement was made which was to have momentous consequences.

And now, at dinner at Hope Vale, on Christmas evening, he was again talking over his plans with the baroness.

'Morton will call here for me after dinner,' said he, 'and we are going to ride to Montego Bay. If we find anything untoward or threatening we are going to speak to the people. Morton is known to be a kind slave-owner, Psyche, and it must have already become known for miles and miles that I have manumitted my slaves on Plimsole.'

'You are right, darling,' said she, 'but take care of yourself; keep out of trouble as much as you can.'

'You to say this!' he laughed.

'Yes,' she replied; 'for I know quite well that your chief motive for this mission is to save me from any annoyance or danger. But you must remember yourself also, darling. After all, what I have done I have done with my eyes wide open. It was right, and I do not regret it.'

She ceased, and then there broke from her a piteous cry :
'Fred, wasn't I right? Tell me, do you think I have done
wrong?'

He looked at her misty eyes. 'You are the most courageous
woman I have ever known, dear,' he said, knowing that
now she was thinking only of his safety. 'Worry about
nothing. In this matter we stand firmly together, sink or
swim. Ah, there is Morton now, I hear him riding this
way.'

Christopher Morton came into the house but for one drink
of Christmas cheer, and then the two men rode away. A
heaviness as of doom seemed suddenly to descend upon the
baroness. For the first time since her advent in Jamaica
she sank upon a chair, pressed her face against her hands,
and sobbed as though her heart would break.

Chapter 24

THE TERRIBLE LAUGH

'He came to my house early this morning,' said Mr. Buxton to the baroness; 'he asked me to tell you that he and Mr. Morton would be going about the parish today, but that he hoped to see you this evening. I think, milady, that Mr. O'Brian and Mr. Morton are somewhat alarmed.'

'It may be so, Buxton,' answered the baroness abstractedly; 'but we cannot know until Wednesday, can we?'

'Yes, milady, we can know now. I know, for instance, that our people will be at work on Wednesday; they are full of gratitude and joy. But I am sure that not one slave will be seen on most of the other estates in this parish.'

'What is to be will be,' she replied wearily, 'but I was hoping of late that we might pass through this crisis without bloodshed. You don't think that is now possible, Buxton?'

'No,' replied the old man. 'I know the people, both the whites and the blacks. Nothing will now induce the white men to desist from insisting that Sunday forms a part of the annual Christmas holidays for the slaves, and even if they yielded on this point, nothing would induce most of the slaves to refrain from rebelling for their freedom at the end of the holiday. When do you leave St. James, milady?'

'Some time next week, I believe, Buxton—if ever,' she added as an afterthought, and then repeated under her breath, 'if ever.'

'Leave as soon as you can,' implored Buxton earnestly. 'I don't see why you should not start for Kingston today with a sufficient armed escort of your own people. What is to keep you here? You have been very kind to every man and woman on this estate. You have given the people freedom; my son and I thank you that you have legally made us the attorneys for Hope Vale until your son comes of age. What is to keep you here, where there may be so much trouble, where there is going to be so much trouble?'

'I cannot leave Mr. O'Brian, Buxton,' answered the baroness sadly. 'Are you not thinking of him too?'

'No, milady, no, for he is a man, and a white man, and can well look after himself.'

'But you know that I am going to marry him, Buxton?'

'Yes, and therefore he should be willing to start with you for Kingston this evening when he comes to see you; if he cares for you, milady, as I believe he does, he will not hesitate about that.' Buxton spoke with a stubborn look on his face.

'Do you think Mr. O'Brian is of the kind that runs away from danger?' questioned the baroness gently.

Buxton made no reply; he felt that argument was futile. It was early morning; he had come over to the Great House from his residence to give to the baroness the message left with him by Frederick O'Brian himself. This was Monday; he doubted whether any blow would be struck by slave or slave-owner before the next day had completely passed; but he believed that on Wednesday hell would flame forth in the parish. And looking now in the face of the baroness he perceived that, in spite of her words suggesting a hope to the contrary, she realised it also.

Clothed in cool white, she accompanied Buxton to the front door of the Great House, stood on the stone platform on which the flight of steps terminated, and watched him stride towards his house. 'A good man,' she thought, 'and a true man; I wonder what he was in his youth? I wonder what sort of woman was his wife. I wonder if there are many like him in this country. Perhaps persons like myself may be thinking today that all these men of the dominant class —for, after all, he does belong to the dominant class in

Jamaica—are evil from their hearts outward, are simply beasts in human disguise; and yet we may be mistaken. It is true that only God can judge what man or woman really is.'

She was startled to find that she had been thinking so reverentially, with such an implicit faith, of Almighty God. She was largely the inheritor of eighteenth-century scepticism; she had hardly thought or spoken of God in all her days. But now it was all different; something deep within her stirred and turned her feelings and thoughts from the purely mundane aspect of affairs. 'Perhaps,' she reflected, 'I may be dead before this week ends. I wonder, if that happened, what would become of Fred in the years to come? I hope that God will help him.'

Someone—wasn't it old Psyche Huntingdon?—had said some time ago that Frederick was living with some woman or other; but the baroness had never hinted at that to him. The woman, if she really existed, certainly did not live at Plimsole, and there never had been a suggestion of children. Perhaps the connection, if it had existed, had ended once Frederick had come to know her. This was the implicit opinion of the baroness. It happened to be true.

In the evening Fred himself rode up to the Great House; it had been dark for some time, although the hour was yet early. The December dusk had rapidly deepened into darkness; in most other country houses of the wealthy, dinner had already been despatched; but this meal had been purposely delayed at Hope Vale by the baroness in the hope that Frederick would arrive in time to share it.

He did; and she was waiting for him on the front porch as he rode up. 'Buxton told me you were coming, Fred,' she cried, 'and I have waited dinner for you. When you have washed up we will dine and then you can tell me all about your adventures during the day.'

In the dining-room with all the candles in the chandelier lighted, and all the candles in the sconces against the walls,

and with the huge mahogany dining-table covered with
viands in the Jamaica fashion—a profusion of them, a
waste of them, but something that could not possibly be
avoided unless one sought the reputation of being parsi-
monious—Frederick O'Brian told his tale. There was not
much, after all, to say. He and Christopher Morton had
ridden over a fair expanse of the parish that day and would
continue their self-imposed mission on the morrow. Almost
everywhere, amongst the crowds of slaves on the roads as
well as in Montego Bay, they had noticed the defiant
attitude of the people. 'And,' added Frederick, 'there was
something about them that I had never observed before.'

'Yes?' interposed the baroness anxiously.

'Yes. Again and again I heard the women in the crowds
burst into peals of shrill, blood-curdling laughter. I shuddered. Morton too was disturbed at that. He told me that
it was the prelude to the signal of blood violence. Only
when in a certain frame of mind do they shriek and laugh
like that. They are already drunk with blood-lust, Psyche.
Nothing will stop them now.'

'About the slave-owners, Fred; you saw some of them
too?'

'Yes, we called at Crumley for lunch; you know Crumley
is one of the Great Houses just outside Montego Bay.
The family were there; there were half a dozen other
persons who had been invited to spend the day. They
greeted Morton and myself coldly, so coldly that we should
have left at once had we not had a definite purpose in mind.
We wanted to talk to the owner of Crumley about the folly
of insisting that Sunday should count as one of the usual
Christmas holidays of the slaves. But feeling ran too high
in that house, the expressions we heard were too bitter:
we thought it best to say little or nothing. Maybe they knew
why Morton and myself were there: they must have learnt
about our attitude. In any case the decision expressed was
emphatic. The slaves would have to consider yesterday as

one of the three days to which they were entitled, they said, and every man and woman not reporting for work on Wednesday morning would be flogged. What can you do with people like those, Psyche? Or with almost any of the people here? Although I have long been in this island, I suddenly feel myself a stranger and an alien. I feel that I have nothing in common with the people of Jamaica.'

'And yet you are going to continue to ride about the parish tomorrow and try to persuade these men and women against their will?'

'There is nothing else to do except quit and run,' he answered. 'And I do not think you would like me to quit and run, even were I so inclined, my dear.'

'No,' she replied proudly. 'You are an O'Brian, and Morton comes of an English family whom no one has ever yet accused of cowardice; and I—well, after all, Fred, on my father's side I am a Huntingdon you know.'

'And could be no more a Huntingdon than on your father's or your mother's side, Psyche,' he riposted swiftly, 'unless your mother were also a Huntingdon.'

'But, Fred——' she waved to the domestics lingering behind their chairs and listening intently; these left the room with obvious reluctance.

'Fred,' she resumed (and she dropped her voice to a half whisper), 'there is something I must tell you before it is too late. I am a Huntingdon, yes, there can be no doubt as to my paternity. But do you understand that my mother was captured and brought to this island from Africa, is still alive, and is living not far from us here? Her name is Psyche Huntingdon, Fred, and you have met her. Buxton must know the facts and Morton knows them too. I am illegitimate, Fred: you must know that before you marry me.'

'Who told you all this?' he demanded quickly.

'No one. But the truth was there for me to read. I know it now.'

'And I have known it for some time, Psyche,' he laughed;

'don't you think that much of other people's business is known to everyone in Jamaica after a little while? Oh, my dear, you have been the subject of conversation in half the parishes of the island within the last few weeks; but in England you and I will be taken at our true human valuation, and I know that your value there will be looked upon as greater than mine.'

He rose at once, to prevent any rejoinder on her part. Tears of gratitude had sprung to her eyes, had overflowed; he bent towards her and wiped them away with his handkerchief; then on her lips he kissed her passionately. 'And now I must ride to Plimsole,' he said, 'for I promised to meet Christopher Morton there.'

He paused as he reached the front door.

'I don't think you will see me tomorrow,' he said, 'and perhaps not on Wednesday either. After that——'

She clung to him speechless. And thus they parted.

In the afternoon of the following day, Tuesday, the baroness was aroused from her usual siesta by a clamour in front of the Great House. One of the servants rushed in to tell her that the 'sets' were dancing in front of the house, and craved her recognition. The people of Hope Vale belonged to the Blue faction of the 'sets', the slaves from some neighbouring plantation were evidently Reds, and these were dancing in rivalry in the grounds of Hope Vale. She went outside; she observed a capering, prancing crowd, some of the members of which were clothed in blue, some in red, some of the men wearing the horns of a bull on their heads, and with masked faces: all uttering discordant cries, all moving and dancing as though possessed of tireless energy to the sound of their improvised drums and fifes. She watched them awhile, smiling, then threw a handful of small silver coins amongst them. She knew that this was expected of her, and would mark the end of the entertainment.

It seemed to her that the minds of these people were fixed wholly on their dancing, and perhaps on the feasting that was to follow, when an ominous sound fell on her ear. Two bands had been formed, Reds and Blues keeping rigidly to themselves now when prepared to leave the plantation; but while the Blues, the people of Hope Vale, were still laughing, there was a sudden silence amongst the Reds; and as these moved away two or three women lifted their voices in a piercing, mirthless laugh that might have been heard great distances away. Never had such a sound assailed the hearing of the baroness in her life; instantly she remembered what Frederick O'Brian had said about the terrible laughter amongst some of the crowds that Christopher Morton and himself had ridden past on the previous day. She blenched, but she refused to give way to any access of fear. She was a woman of action. She acted now to the best of her ability and knowledge.

She despatched a bearer to Cowbend to ask that Mashimba's son, young Charles Huntingdon, should be sent to her immediately. Within an hour he arrived, having ridden hell-for-leather from Cowbend. Briefly she gave him her orders. Montego Bay, she knew, would be the focus of news during the next few days; Charles was therefore commanded to go that day to Montego Bay to put up at some place there, and to ride immediately to Hope Vale if he should hear anything affecting Mr. O'Brian or Mr. Morton. Charles understood his instructions completely; that afternoon he was stationed in Montego Bay, which wore an odd expression of expectancy and tension. He knew that tonight the slaves on the different estates in the island must return to the estates, by midnight at latest, or declare by their action that they were openly in rebellion. As a free man, what the slaves did affected him not at all; as boss of the few on Cowbend—for Psyche Huntingdon, the 'ex-nurse,' had on some pretext or other not yet set free her slaves—he was secretly inclined to side with the slave-owners and not with those who clamoured for immediate emancipation. But he knew that the baroness had declared for freedom at once, and so he kept his views and his feelings to himself. He was to be her ears in Montego Bay. To that duty he would be faithful to the end.

Chapter 25

FREDERICK

IT HAD come.

It was Wednesday morning; the baroness herself had
ridden round part of Hope Vale with Mr. Buxton and his
son, and had seen that her people at any rate were at work.
But there was uneasiness amongst them, and unrest; very
few of them indeed could set their minds to any tasks that
had to be undertaken. At any moment they might cease
from any pretence of labour.

Enquiries had elicited the fact that only on this property,
on Plimsole, and on one or two others in the parish (though
these had not manumitted their slaves) were the people at
work; throughout the parish—and throughout many other
parishes in Jamaica also—there were wholesale desertions
of toilers. The rebellion had begun.

The baroness watched a number of men loading hogsheads of sugar made that month into a wain drawn by six
oxen, the usual means of transportation of the Jamaica
sugar estates. She noticed how little the minds of the
people were on the job they were handling; how excited
was their expression, how anxious their looks. Buxton
noticed it also; so did his son. They knew that the workers
had turned out that day only because of gratitude. Much
would evidently not be accomplished during the rest of the
week. To expect that would be to expect too much of
Jamaica human nature.

The baroness beckoned Buxton away with a wave of her
whip and then rode slowly in the direction of the Great
House.

'You will not get much work out of the people today,' she said to him, and at once he agreed.

'But it is better that they should feel that they are expected to work,' he said, 'than that they should be allowed to wander as they please about the roads of St. James. For then they might get into bad company, and presently we'd be hearing that they were in trouble.'

'You will soon be hearing,' she said a little bitterly, 'that there would be no rebellion in Jamaica but for me.'

'Now, that is what I do not think, milady,' he answered; 'not now. I have been giving my mind to this matter, and have also been talking it over with one or two other folk. Even before you came to Jamaica the belief was gaining ground that Emancipation was coming at the end of this year, that the King of England had made the slaves of Jamaica free. And when you talked to some of the leaders of this rebellion, they had already made up their minds as to what they were going to do. I do not say you haven't encouraged them, in a manner of speaking, but you could not possibly have stopped them. Make yourself easy on that score.'

'What follows from that, Buxton?'

'Well, this at least. Even those planters who would wish to say you were the cause of all the worry we are going to have cannot possibly bring such a charge against you. I have no doubt they have already sent to Kingston to tell the Government what is happening here, and in a very short time you will see Martial Law proclaimed in this part of the island. But no military or civil tribunal, milady, is going to interfere with you.'

'I am not thinking of my own safety, Buxton.'

'I don't think you are; but I am, and I am sure Mr. O'Brian is. And we both will be very glad to know you are safe.'

'Well,' she smiled faintly, as they reached the Great House, 'I think that to encourage people in what has turned

out to be a rebellion is a criminal offence, though I do not
regret it for a moment. But I am not so safe after all, you
see.'

'Perhaps. But with me and Mr. O'Brian to swear that
you really had nothing to do with this business, and with
Mr. Morton and other persons to swear it, too, it would
take more than a few outsiders to implicate you.'

Buxton spoke positively. And she knew what he meant.
He and others were prepared, if needs be, to perjure themselves on her behalf!

The long day dragged on. Blue and beautiful, the skies
soft and luminous, the December heat not unbearable at
the warmest hours of the day, there was yet a feeling of
tension everywhere. The evening came, and darkness; the
baroness sat in an armchair within the Great House, hoping
to hear Frederick's voice at any moment, yet remembering
his message that she was not likely to see him on Wednesday
as well as Tuesday. Then she heard a rap at the front door,
and went and opened it herself. Mr. Buxton was standing
there, and the first words he uttered indicated the strong
emotion under which he was labouring.

'Look, baroness,' he cried, and his right arm stabbed the
air in several directions. But she had already seen. Far
away in some instances, nearer at hand in others, fires were
blazing on the surrounding heights. Even as she stared some
of them gathered volume and leapt higher and more
fiercely. She uttered not a word.

'You know what they are?' murmured Buxton.

'I can guess,' she said.

'They are Great Houses or sugar works blazing,' he went
on; 'I think they are sugar houses mainly, though I am
certain that some residences are going to be destroyed by
the slaves tonight.'

'And the families in those residences, Buxton?'

'Most of them must have already fled for refuge to the

town,' he answered; 'they must have known what was coming.'

'I have no place to flee to,' she said.

'And no need to fly,' said Buxton. 'You know, milady, I didn't agree with the manumission of your slaves at first; but now I think you were right. Freedom has to come; we have all known this for some time. Those who have taken time by the forelock, or who have treated their slaves kindly, as we have always done on Hope Vale, will have workers enough in the future. Those fires show what may be expected of the foolish or indifferent.'

'So at long last you agree that I was right, my friend,' said the baroness. 'From my heart I thank you for your words.'

She held out her hand to him; he pressed it and left for his own house. He was heart-glad that no part of Hope Vale had been given to the flames.

In the darkness of the night the young woman, feeling strangely sad and lonely, looked about her. Fire after fire blazed on the encircling horizon; lurid, ominous, they seemed a fiery threat screamed forth by the slaves; it was as though a great knell were sounding over the whole parish, the whole island, as though the fires so fiercely burning in the distance were a sign and indication of the purging that had already begun.

She slept fitfully that night; was up early the next morning: this was Thursday, and she expected to hear something from Frederick O'Brian. He must have done all that he could on Tuesday and Wednesday to warn the Negroes against madness and violence, to plead with the slave-owners for leniency, intelligent action and justice. He had failed; it was fated that he and Morton must fail. But now they could return to their respective homes, knowing that at least they had done their best, that at least they had left nothing untried.

It was about nine o'clock in the forenoon that she heard

a horse being furiously ridden towards the Great House. The sound stopped for a while at Mr. Buxton's residence, was then resumed, and in a few minutes Mashimba's son, Charles, was rapping loudly at one of the back doors of the Great House, calling for admission. A frightened servant brought him to the baroness. She looked at his face and read there grief and consternation. Her heart sank.

'What is it, Charles?' she gasped.

'Mr. O'Brian and Mr. Morton, ma'am,' he stammered, then stopped.

'Well?'

'I hear they was riding into Montego Bay early this morning when them met a lot of the rebels. The rebels didn't know who they were, and shot them dead, milady. Some gentlemen an' their slaves going to Montego Bay found the bodies an' took them to the Bay. They are in the Court House now, and they making coffins for them. They send already to Mr. Morton's property and to Plimsole to tell them what happened, and I come to tell you.'

She had been standing with one hand resting on a table; now she leaned heavily on the table, feeling that if she moved she would stagger and fall. An intense silence prevailed for many moments, then she whispered, 'Are you certain Mr. O'Brian has been killed, Charles?'

'Yes, missis,' answered the boy sobbing; 'they allow me to go into the Montego Bay Court House and I saw the body.'

Another spell of silence. It seemed to her indeed as though the very wind had fallen suddenly, that the trees were standing still to hear the tidings Charles had brought. It seemed to her something within her breast had turned to lead. And an icy chilliness pervaded her frame. Fred dead! This was the end of his effort to help others; his effort to help her. Death. Somehow she had never imagined that this would be the conclusion in so far as he was concerned; she had expected to have to fight for her own freedom, but had in her inmost heart believed in her victory should Fred stand at her side. But now, in an instant as it were, a black curtain had rolled down between her present and all the future that she had recently hoped for. She bowed her head; but at once she raised it again, remembering that this news was a call to action by her, that tears must come after. At the moment there was work to be done.

'Charles,' she said, striving to make her voice firm, 'go to Mr. Buxton's house and tell him I want a wain with four strong mules to go at once to Montego Bay to bring Mr. O'Brian to Hope Vale. You have told him already what has happened, haven't you?'

Charles nodded assent.

'Also tell young Mr. Buxton that I want him to go to Montego Bay with you and me at once, and tell Mr. Buxton himself that he must come to me as soon as the wain is ready.' She turned and gave rapid orders to one of her male servants; she herself was going to Montego Bay immediately. Then she passed into her room to don her riding habit. When she was ready the men she had sent for were at the Great House. Both the Buxtons' faces expressed sorrow; but a wise instinct prevented them from uttering a word. They had seen in her face that condolence would now be of no service and most unwelcome.

To the older Buxton she gave instructions as to where Frederick's grave should be dug. 'He will be buried here,' she said with finality, 'not at Plimsole: I will take the responsibility. We will bury him by the river. I think he would have preferred that.'

Charles had changed his mount for a fresh horse; with him and Mr. Buxton's son she set off on her ride to Montego Bay, the four mules and the wain thundering in her rear towards the town.

Montego Bay was full of militia men, who apparently preferred the safety of the town to the perils of the hills where the rebels were believed to be lurking. Strange and varied uniforms marked out the officers of this force; but at any rate families who came seeking refuge in Montego Bay knew that so long as the militia were there the rebels would not dare to attack the place. There had been some attempt at placing sentries on the roads leading to Montego Bay; but the baroness, accompanied by a white and a black retainer, had no difficulty whatever in gaining entrance; following Charles she rode to the Court House, mounted the steps, and passed into the main hall of the building. Four coffins were laid out there, in each of them a body. These bodies had been decently cleansed; on their faces was a look of peace. At the left of the row was one whom she recognised at once. She fell on her knees beside the bier, and kissed with passion the pale cold forehead of her dead lover.

In the room were many planters, men who were waiting for the arrival of the troops from Kingston, some of them commanders of the local militia. Some of them knew who she was, others enquired; some muttered that she was responsible for the troubles that had broken forth, others shook their heads deprecatingly at this suggestion: like Mr. Buxton, they felt that the rebellion would have come in any case. The baroness rose from her knees, and speaking to young Buxton, asked him to employ a few men to take the coffin containing Frederick to the wain outside; but first, she said, the lid must be screwed on. One of the people in the room asked her if she had any authority to move the body. She replied brusquely that she had. The man hesitated—'I was engaged to be married to Mr. O'Brian next week in Kingston,' she said. 'He has no one else but me. Isn't that enough?'

After that no one interfered with her; after all, Frederick O'Brian was dead and evidently was to receive a decent burial. Young Buxton and Charles had got half a dozen men in the street outside the Court House; these at a word from the white man screwed the lid on the coffin, hoisted it on to their shoulders, and began to move slowly out of the room and down the stairs. Dry-eyed, the baroness watched them go, then without glancing to right or left followed them, and rode behind the wain to Hope Vale. The funeral was to follow immediately on the body's arrival at the estate. There could not be a moment's unnecessary delay in this tropical climate.

Few mourners stood around the grave that afternoon; the Buxtons, Psyche Huntingdon, old Mashimba and his son, and the baroness only, with the elder Buxton reading the funeral service. The baroness stood aloof from all the others, and those who watched her immobile face never guessed how terrible was her fight against the inclination to scream aloud her grief to the winds of heaven, to rail at fate, to heap curses at the bitter fortune that was hers. She fought her battle silently, and triumphed over her insurgent emotions, but the struggle was awful, exhausting. Physically and spiritually her strength had almost gone out of her. One sentence only she uttered that indicated how deeply this wound had entered her heart, words that startled those that heard them. 'My grave will lie next to Mr. O'Brian's,' she said. 'Don't forget that I wished for this.'

Chapter 26

AS IT WAS IN THE BEGINNING

THE maids went soft-footed about the house, deep sympathy depicted in every line of their countenances. At times one of them would pause before the closed mahogany door of the baroness's bedroom, believing that she heard within the sound of awful, piteous sobbing. But she dared not rap and make enquiries; and when she sought out some of her companions they too were helpless; all they could do was to allow their emotional nature to have full vent so that they might weep unrestrainedly with the stricken lady who lay in the darkness, sobbing as though her heart would break.

Later on came Mr. Buxton and Psyche Huntingdon to the house. Psyche Huntingdon had been taken by Mr. Buxton to his residence, where she had sat upon a chair on the back veranda, with her head between her hands, motionless, thinking only of the terrible disaster that had come upon her daughter, the daughter whom she had not dared to acknowledge except to those who knew. When it was dark, Mr. Buxton suggested to her that they should walk over to the Great House: 'It may be that the baroness needs some help,' he said; 'anyhow, the least we can do is to offer it.'

It was Buxton who rapped at the bedroom door when they got to the Great House; a voice strained, the voice of a woman who had been weeping, answered, 'Who is that?'

'Psyche Huntingdon and me, milady,' Buxton answered. 'Do you want anything? Can we do anything?'

'No; but both of you may come here tomorrow morning, say at about eight. I shall want to see you then.'

This appointment caused a strange uplifting of the spirits

217

of both Buxton and Psyche; it assured them that the baroness was contemplating nothing desperate immediately or she would hardly have made the appointment. They had never known her to break her word.

A maid whispered something to the old nurse. 'What about dinner, milady?' she asked. 'It is late now, and you haven't eaten anything since morning.'

'One of the maids may bring me some coffee and a few biscuits later,' said the baroness. 'Good night.'

They left then, and half an hour after they had gone the baroness came out of her room, her face set and drawn but with no tears in her eyes, and five minutes after one of the women attached to the house brought in a large coffee pot with coffee, a sugar bowl, a jug of hot cow's milk, fresh butter made on the estate, and bread and biscuits, all tastefully arranged to tempt the baroness's appetite. These things were placed on the table in the dining-room; she sat at the head of the table and ate and drank mechanically, drinking more coffee than was her wont at night but eating very little. 'You have a small coffee mill in this house, haven't you?' she asked the maid when this improvised supper was finished.

'Yes, missis.'

'Bring it with some parched coffee and a spirit stove, and leave them on the sideboard. You may bring some milk and sugar also.'

The maid did as she was bid, and awaited the next order.

'You may all retire now,' said the baroness, 'I want to do some writing. Lock the doors and open the house at seven o'clock tomorrow morning.'

'That is late, milady,' ventured the maid.

'It will be early enough tomorrow, Daphne,' retorted the baroness kindly.

'The lights, missis?' questioned the maid.

'I will see that they are put out,' said the baroness; 'you need worry yourself about nothing.'

Left alone with the outer doors of the Great House all closed and locked, she went to a small escritoire that she had had moved into the dining-room, sat down and commenced to write. It was a long letter that she wrote to her son, addressed to the care of his guardian in England. The letter was not to be handed to the boy until he was sixteen years of age, she stipulated, and in it she told him that he would never see her again, 'for,' she wrote, 'I have fallen a victim to one of the diseases of this country, and am not likely to recover, though this you may not learn for years.' She advised him never to come to Jamaica—what is the sense? she asked. 'What could you do here? Emancipation, freedom, is coming apace. Long before you are sixteen, dearest, perhaps, indeed, next year, there will not be a slave in this country. Hope Vale is in good hands. You may want to sell it when you are of age (as you know, everything I possess has been left to you, this property included, and I do not believe that you will ever want for money). But don't sell the property if young Buxton is still in charge of it and can make it even pay its way without any profit accruing to you; he is a good lad and will prove worthy of your trust.

'I think his father will be dead by then; but one can never tell. I have made arrangements that the old man shall not want if he should retire at any time; but I wish you always to bear him in mind, and his son also.'

There was much more in this letter. Put in an envelope and sealed, it was addressed in firm resolute handwriting and left on the escritoire. The baroness then glanced at the huge clock that relentlessly ticked away the hours on the mahogany sideboard. It registered only ten. She moved to an armchair, placed her right cheek against her hand, the elbow resting on the arm of the chair, and began to think.

So this was the end of it all. As it was in the beginning so was it now: in a way the wheel of her life, begun to revolve so long ago, had come full circle at last. She knew the truth. Josephine Brookfield had died at her mother's hand because, otherwise, she would have taken away Charles Huntingdon, noble in character in his way, a great gentleman, but perhaps the weakest of the male Huntingdons who had ever been born. But for that murder—for murder it was—she herself, the baroness, would never have been born.

She knew that no one remembered Josephine Brookfield now; even Buxton, who might years ago have shuddered at the killing of the youthful white woman, and have been on her side, never gave her a thought in these days; and if he did he would probably assert that what Psyche Huntingdon had done was right. For now he believed in Psyche. In thirty years his mind had probably undergone a complete change and revolution. She felt that Buxton had changed.

He approved of everything her mother had done. He believed that his sable silent co-adjutor, who never had forgotten all these years that he was a white man and entitled to respect, was always right.

But was she right? The years had passed; Psyche Huntingdon had stood but a few hours ago by the grave of the one man the baroness had ever loved, with the sole exception of Charles Baron Huntingdon, her father. Psyche had seen, almost, the end of the circling of the wheel she had set in motion so long ago. The finality was yet to come. And that would be bitterest of all for the unfortunate woman. She would pay to the full. She, at least, would not believe that she had been always right.

But did it matter? wondered the baroness. Did anything matter? Thirty, forty years hence, indeed ten or five years hence, who would think of her, or of her lover, or of any personality connected with this little tragedy of her life? How many indeed would think of it tomorrow? No more surely than a mere handful of persons.

Some words came to her memory; she remembered

having read them years before; in the Bible, she thought. They said that in the hereafter there should be no more sorrow, no more weeping, no more pain. She believed that was true; and all she wanted now was oblivion; she wished to be nothing, nothing. During the last few weeks she had surely suffered more than enough of pain of heart, more than enough of sorrow, and now she knew, as never before in her life had she known, what weeping meant.

She turned her eyes to the sideboard; two hours had passed; it was now midnight. She rose decisively, poured the parched coffee into the little mill, and out of her pocket drew an envelope containing the few withered beans which Psyche Huntingdon had given to her and which had come years before from far-off Africa. Two would be enough, she knew; two had paralysed and then killed a strong calf only the other day: the beans had not lost their terrible potency, perhaps would never lose it. She ground the coffee and the poison beans together, carefully poured the powdered stuff into a metal coffee-pot with water, and placed the pot on the spirit stove to boil. When it was ready she drained off the liquid, put into it milk and sugar and slowly drank it: it was badly made, muddy. There was another cup of coffee left; that also she drank; then the few remaining poison beans she took, and, one by one, she hurled each of them out of a separate window of the dining-room with all the strength of her arm. They were tiny shrivelled things, they never would be found she was convinced. As to the envelope that had contained them for so many years, that was torn to little pieces, and held in the palm of her hand outside an open window to be wafted away by the cold, strongly-blowing December wind.

The coffee prevented her from sleeping; but she did not wish to sleep. She still had thinking to do, her past to review, her happy past in England, for even when her husband had died she had felt no terrible sorrow such as affected her now when she thought of Fred O'Brian lying in his grave so near to the Hope Vale river, separated from her for ever so long, she thought, as she was alive. A happy youth, and then this! Was it for this she had been born? And poor, unhappy Fred?

It was midnight now; she too should be dead some time after midday tomorrow. In the afternoon they would bury her, or on the following morning at latest. And she would lie by Fred, and in time to come the very site of their graves would be forgotten.

She would not live without him; she knew he was the only man she had ever loved, would ever love. Poor Fred; weak perhaps, but noble at heart and a gentleman, and dying in a noble cause with another man who also stood superior to the men about him. A gentleman to the last moment of his life.

So she thought, forgetting to extinguish the candles until most of them burnt down to their metal sockets, then guttered loudly and went out. And so the hours passed until through the open windows to the east she saw the sky lighten, the stars dimmed, and opaline and rosy streaks appear. The glow of morning was spreading over the earth. Another day had dawned. Then she noticed that her legs were growing heavy. The poison was taking effect. But there was no pain.

At seven o'clock the servants began to open the doors of the Great House; one of the maids coming in with brush and wax to polish the floor of the dining-room was startled to find the baroness in an armchair staring before her. The maid hurried to her side, thinking that perhaps she had fallen asleep and had just been awakened.

Quite clearly the baroness spoke to her: 'I am very ill, Phyllis; I think I am dying. Miss Psyche and Marse Buxton are coming here at eight o'clock; if you like you can go and tell them to come now.'

The maid uttered a shriek which brought others hurrying into the room; then she rushed off to Mr. Buxton's place to tell him what the baroness had said. Very soon Buxton and Psyche Huntingdon appeared at the Great House, panting with exertion; they had run most of the way. Psyche fell on her knees beside the baroness, 'Oh, God,' she cried, 'what is the matter, me darling? The girl said you were dying.'

Buxton, after one glance at the baroness, had hurried outside and had ordered one of the men-servants to rush over to his house and tell his son to ride hell-for-leather to the Bay and bring a doctor—two doctors if he could get them—'And tell him he must go at once,' the father added. Buxton then returned to the dining-room to hear the baroness speaking to Psyche Huntingdon.

'Yes,' said the baroness, a little while after the old woman had spoken, 'yes, I am dying, of the same means that Josephine Brookfield died of, Mother—for I know that you are my mother, have known it for some time now. This is no time for any further pretence; let us face the truth. I am dying, but there is no pain. And I have no regrets. Maybe it was fated that I should die like this; perhaps it is just as well. Your doctor will come,' said she, raising her eyes slowly to Buxton; 'but will perhaps say that I died of heart failure or something of the sort, brought on by the slaying of Frederick O'Brian. I do not think he will be very wrong, if we look at the ultimate cause of my death. Had Fred lived, I should have wanted to live also; I do not want to live now that he is dead.'

She ceased to speak, and the others watched her. Psyche Huntingdon knew that there was nothing that could be done to save her now; Buxton felt helpless; the men and women of Hope Vale, amongst whom the news had in some mysterious way spread rapidly, gathered weeping about the building, while some of them whispered that the spirit of Frederick O'Brian had come to take her with him so that in death they should not be divided. It was towards midday that she fell into a coma. In another few hours she was dead.

Early on the following morning those who had stood around the grave of Frederick O'Brian consigned the body of the Baroness de Brion to the earth; though on this occasion a clergyman from Montego Bay read the funeral service, and not Mr. Buxton, as on the day before. Meanwhile, in England, a lusty little boy laughed and played, enjoying the winter's cold and the flakes of snow that fell at intervals, revelling in all that was beautiful about him, and giving not a thought to the mother who, at that moment, was lying forever still in a far-away Jamaica grave.

THE END